The gallery storefront glass shattered as gunshots rang out...

Suddenly, Luci felt a hand yank her to the floor. She landed on Bard's hard chest, and he quickly rolled over and shielded her from the unrelenting bullets flying by.

"Looks like your friend is back," he said through gritted teeth. The constant discharge of ammo told her this was not a handgun like before. "And this time, he's not leaving until the job is done."

This guy was out for blood. The viciousness of the shoot-up told Bard this was personal. Whoever this was wanted Luci dead.

But why?

The shooting stopped, and a strange silence filled the atmosphere. A few hanging pieces of glass let go and shattered to the floor in the aftermath. Bard knew he had to get Luci out before he heard footsteps crunching over the destruction.

He shifted away from her and whispered, "Get to the back door. Stay low."

When she hesitated, he said, "Don't look back. Just go..."

Katy Lee writes suspenseful romances that thrill and inspire. She believes every story should stir and satisfy the reader—from the edge of their seat. A native New Englander, Katy loves to knit warm woolly things. She enjoys traveling the side roads and exploring the locals' hideaways. A homeschooling mom of three competitive swimmers, Katy often writes from the stands while cheering them on. Visit Katy at katyleebooks.com.

Books by Katy Lee

Love Inspired Suspense

Warning Signs
Grave Danger
Sunken Treasure
Permanent Vacancy
Amish Country Undercover
Amish Sanctuary
Holiday Suspect Pursuit
Cavern Cover-Up
Santa Fe Setup

Roads to Danger

Silent Night Pursuit
Blindsided
High Speed Holiday

Visit the Author Profile page at LoveInspired.com for more titles.

SANTA FE SETUP

KATY LEE

LOVE INSPIRED SUSPENSE
INSPIRATIONAL ROMANCE

LOVE INSPIRED® SUSPENSE
INSPIRATIONAL ROMANCE

ISBN-13: 978-1-335-58749-7

Santa Fe Setup

Copyright © 2022 by Katherine Lee

Recycling programs
for this product may
not exist in your area.

For questions and comments about the quality of this book, please contact us
at CustomerService@Harlequin.com.

Love Inspired
22 Adelaide St. West, 41st Floor
Toronto, Ontario M5H 4E3, Canada
www.LoveInspired.com

Printed in U.S.A.

While we look not at the things which are seen, but at the things which are not seen: for the things which are seen are temporal; but the things which are not seen are eternal.
—*2 Corinthians* 4:18

To Jason.

Keep looking up. Your help comes from the Lord.

ONE

Luci Butler was a thief. Albeit a cute one, but still a thief. And she was also being followed by someone other than him.

Bard Holland slunk his large frame lower behind the steering wheel, doing his best to remain inconspicuous as he watched his friend's younger sister steal a painting right off the wall of Santa Fe's prestigious Salazar Art Gallery. Her stalker was packing heat, and as an investigator for the Bureau of Land Management, Bard knew people generally only brought guns if they were willing to use them. He wondered if at some point Luci had ripped this lowlife off as easily as she lifted that painting and carried it out the front door.

Or perhaps this guy had been hired by Darral Lindsay, the fugitive Luci's brother had recently outed as a criminal down at Carlsbad Caverns National Park. Darral and his crime family had more money than Bard would ever see in his lifetime and hiring a hitman to pick off Truman Butler's family in revenge would barely be a drop in the bucket for the man, even with the federal government seizing all his assets. Tru may be a park ranger and not law enforcement, but when crime came to his national park, he put a stop to it. But he also put his life in danger. As well as the woman in his life.

But that didn't mean this stalker following Luci was working for Darral Lindsay as retribution. Bard didn't want to jump to conclusions and decided only to focus on the evidence at hand. With Luci Butler stealing a painting, perhaps she had a secret sinister life her brother didn't know about.

In the few conversations Bard had had with Tru about his sister, he'd described her to a T. The twenty-six-year-old barely reached five feet and had short black hair in a pixie cut. Tru had once said his little sister's style of clothing was a painting smock. But tonight, she wore all black, right down to her black shoes made for running. If Luci was a painter herself, she would know the value of the piece she just lifted.

That didn't mean Bard was going to let her take a bullet for it, though. He owed Tru too much to let something like that happen to his sister, regardless of her sticky fingers.

Bard kept his eyes locked on the man in the black hoodie. Skinny guy, six feet, face shielded beneath the hood. White hands. Hands that were reaching for his gun as Luci came around the corner of the storefront.

It was go time.

"Stay," he commanded his Belgian Malinois in the back seat of his unmarked car.

Bard pulled the door handle and pushed hard. He had his own gun drawn and ready to take the shooter out. "Hold it right there," he ordered in his most lethal cop voice.

Both the shooter and Luci froze.

Then ran…in different directions.

Bard made a split-second decision. As Luci took off one way, and the stalker in the other, he went after her.

The young woman was fast on her feet, so much lighter than himself who had to carry over six feet of bulk muscle. Even with the framed painting tucked under her arm, she managed to stay ahead.

"Luci," he called out.

The spring in her step faltered, and she looked over her shoulder at him. But she never stopped running.

"You're in danger. I'm here to help you."

"It's mine!" she shouted back and picked up her steps to run faster. She turned the corner at the next intersection, and when he made it there, she was gone.

Poof, as though she had evaporated.

Bard slowed to a walk, scanning the dark streets in front of him. There was one lamppost at the end, and she could have snuck into any of the shadows between here and there. Santa Fe Plaza at night was fairly quiet, given that most of the shops closed down around six. Being that it was after midnight, the place felt desolate. Bard looked around for a patrol car before he continued down the street. He'd have loved to send the local law enforcement in the direction of the stalker. Right now, his only choice was to find Luci and convince her she was in danger.

Bard passed by tan stucco walls of box-shaped buildings with brown wooden doors as he moved away from the two-story storefronts. Off in the distance, he heard the start of a car engine with the squeal of tires immediately following.

Luci was on the run again.

But at least she was still alive…for now. Her stalker could be right on her tail.

Bard turned and raced around the corner to get back to his car. He had one home address for her, but when he went there earlier in the day, the neighbor said she moved out a week ago. The neighbor gave him the address of Salazar Art Gallery as her place of employment. He shouldn't be surprised an art thief would choose to work at an art gallery. Easy access to the goods.

But then, she did say, *It's mine!* Had she been talking about the painting? In the moment of chasing her down, he only had one thing on his mind: protecting her from someone who meant her harm.

And he hadn't even done that right.

Bard raced toward his car, thinking of the last time he let his friend down…and nearly got him killed. Taking the transfer to the Santa Fe BLM office had more to do with failing Tru than the city's need for an investigator. Bard had never doubted his investigative instincts before Tru's case. He'd thought some time in Santa Fe would fix the lapse he'd had at Carlsbad. He had jumped to conclusions about who could be trusted, and he had chosen wrong. His choice put people in more danger. If Tru's sister ended up with a bullet in her tonight, he will have failed Tru again.

And just might need to rethink his line of employment.

Up until tonight, Luci Butler had never stolen anything in her life. If she had taken the painting yesterday, she still wouldn't have. Yesterday, the painting belonged to her. Today, it did not.

She glanced in the rearview mirror to where the framed portrait took up most of the back seat. She also saw a set of headlights speeding her way. It had to be the big, burly man who had chased her down in the Plaza.

Had Sal hired security to guard the gallery?

She supposed as the owner of Salazar Art Gallery, he had every right. She floored her gas pedal, not wanting to find out what the guard would do if he caught her. Would Sal cancel her commissions? Luci bit back a wail at the thought. She had finally been selling her paintings and making some money off them. Not enough to pay the rent at her apartment, but she at least could still afford her small art studio. Letting her apartment go hurt, but not as much as losing her studio would. It was more important to be in the artist district of Santa Fe where she had better opportunities to sell her art. Plus, it was more of a home than she'd had since she was fourteen years old, even if all she had was a couch to sleep on. With her art surrounding her, she didn't feel invisible anymore.

Luci kept her eyes on the dark road ahead of her. She took the twists and turns out of the shopping district and headed for Old Santa Fe where she now lived and worked. But as she approached the next intersection, a car sped through a red light and stopped in the middle of the road.

Luci slammed on the brakes, screeching her tires along the pavement and fishtailing the rear of her car until it finally came to a stop just a few feet from the driver's door.

Then the door opened and out stepped a tall man in a black hoodie.

Another guard?

This was ridiculous. Her paintings weren't a Dalí or an O'Keeffe. Salazar Art Gallery's security was taking this too far.

Before she could say anything, the man pulled out a

gun and pointed it at her. Luci froze at the sight of the dark barrel. Her throat went dry. Her hands gripped the steering wheel as if to hold on during the hit coming her way.

But why? Was this guy really serious? All because of a painting? That *she* painted?

"Give me the painting," the man ordered, his voice like a serrated edge, while his face remained in the shadows of his hood.

It *was* about the painting!

Something in Luci boiled to the top. Even with the gun pointed at her, she threw her car into Park and jumped from the vehicle. "I was going to put the painting back in the morning. Holding a gun on me and nearly making me crash my car into yours is so unnecessary. You could have got us both killed." She opened the back door, doing her best to ignore the gun still on her. Her hands trembled as she pulled the rear door wide. Then she saw the car that had been tailing her driving at full speed toward her. Would he crash right into her too?

Luci dived to the floor of her car as the other car screamed to a stop beside hers. The same giant of a man who had chased her in the Plaza jumped out with his own gun drawn.

Two guns on her now! Wasn't this overkill? All for a painting by a nobody. All because she was a perfectionist with her work and just had to fix something on it. After a life of never being in control and left to feel invisible, Luci had found a way to take back some of her lost control. A canvas gave her free reign over every stroke…something these guys were now trying to take from her.

"Drop your weapon!" the blond-haired giant yelled from behind the side of his car.

Luci peeked up to see he held out his weapon like on the police TV shows. Was he a cop? The thought made her wonder if she would be arrested and sent to jail tonight.

Great, more for her parents to fight over.

Gunshots cracked through the dark night, making this whole scene even deadlier than a moment ago. Luci covered her head and dropped down farther into the back floor of her car. Her legs curled up into a fetal position, and she closed her eyes to the terror going on outside the open door. If she could reach the handle, she would close it. But honestly, she wasn't sure she could move a muscle. Her bravado at standing up to the first guy dissipated with the real sounds of bullets flying.

There was also a dog barking from somewhere close by. It sounded like the large variety, by its deep woof, and it wanted out.

"Stop right there!" the big man shouted, and she heard footsteps running, followed by the roar of an engine that grew quieter as it drove off.

The next moment, Luci saw the big man by her door. "It's safe to come out."

She could still hear the dog barking ferociously. "Is that your dog?"

"Do you have drugs in here?" came his reply.

Luci sputtered at such a question. "Absolutely not."

The man shrugged and looked over his beefy shoulder. Then he turned back to her. "Hero says otherwise."

"Hero?"

"My retired drug-sniffing dog. Hero says you've got

drugs on you, and Hero is never wrong. You're in a lot of trouble, Luci. Why don't you let me help you?"

"Why should I trust you?" she asked cautiously.

"Because you're in danger, and your brother would want me to help you. Expect it even."

She pushed up to sit on the edge of the seat. "No, thank you. I can get by on my own. I've been doing it long enough." She stepped out from the car and waited for him to move to get out of her way. She had to look up, then look higher. She barely came to his chest, and she knew he could pick her up and move her if he wanted to.

The man's hazel eyes glittered with determination and something else she couldn't decipher. She watched his blond facial scruff indent along his jawline as he took a deep breath. As he let it out, she expected him to do something rash.

Instead, he stepped back.

Luci let her own breath out on a sigh and shut the rear door to move into the driver's seat.

"Luci." He spoke quietly behind her. She stopped at his use of her name "You really are in danger, whether from that guy who just held a gun on you or from someone who hired him. If it's connected to the case your brother just had this criminal could be coming after you for revenge. He won't stop until he succeeds."

Luci paused with her hand on the handle. As she stood in indecision, the man's dog continued to bark from the rear seat of the other car. "I need to call my brother to make sure he really knows you. And you need to calm your dog down. I don't have any drugs. Perhaps Hero's getting old."

Bard huffed but nodded. "Make your call. I'll stand guard right here in case that guy comes back."

Luci stepped into her car and sat down. She grabbed her cell phone from the cup holder. "You didn't tell me which brother." She had two and neither would put her at the top of the list to call and warn. She was always the one to call.

"Truman."

Luci knew her brother Tru had just been through a dangerous situation. He didn't tell her the details, as was his typical fashion of keeping her in the dark. If this guy knew the details, then maybe she was in danger. And it had nothing to do with stealing her painting.

She hit the button to call her brother.

Four rings later, it went to voice mail. Luci left a message for Tru to call her. She mentioned his friend stopped by. She looked up at the man, raising her eyebrows in question of who he was.

"Bard Holland, investigator for the Bureau of Land Management, and I arrived just in time."

Whether she trusted him or not, that part was true. "Your friend Bard thinks I'm in danger. If you agree, call me back." She disconnected and put down the phone.

"And if he doesn't agree, you'll what? Let that guy shoot you next time? Because he's coming back, Luci. I know how these criminals work. You can count on it."

TWO

Bard admitted that there could be a gray area between black and white, but he'd only seen it once during his line of work. Most times, he was able to size up a criminal in an instant. So why was he struggling with Luci Butler? It could be because this cute little spitfire, with short black hair and lashes so long, made him forget his train of thought. He needed to focus on why he had come to Santa Fe, and that was to protect her, even if he had to do it from afar. In fact, it was probably best if he did keep his distance.

Bard found himself being pulled in three separate directions as he stood on the corner of a deserted four-way intersection in the dead of night. More than anything, he hated letting the gunman escape, but leaving Luci alone wasn't an option. The third pull was Hero, his dog. Bard needed to tend to him and see what got him so riled up. He wasn't a working dog anymore, but that didn't mean his training disappeared. Hero smelled drugs, and whether Luci admitted it or not, she had some on her. Being that his office had no jurisdiction on the streets of Santa Fe, there wasn't much he could do about that. Not that he would take her in. His friendship with Tru was strained enough.

"Luci, I'd like to get you out of here and someplace safe. That guy could come back anytime, and most likely with reinforcements. These people don't work alone."

Hero banged against the door from inside the car, his barking still just as loud as before.

"How about you just tend to your dog." Luci had her hand on the door handle as if she intended to pull it closed on him.

"I meant what I said. I need to get you someplace safe. Give me a moment with him. But honestly, he won't stop until the drugs are removed from his presence."

She shrugged. "Well, I can't help him with that. I've already told you his sniffer is wrong."

"I'm not accusing you of anything. You don't understand the power these people have. They could have easily planted something in your car. After the case involving your brother, they'll be out for blood."

She frowned, pressing her lips tight in obvious irritation. "If Tru would share, I might know something about that. But he keeps me in the dark about everything. I have to constantly beg him to pick up the phone to call me. And no one has been in my car." She looked up to face him. "An investigator for the Bureau of Land Management. What is that exactly? Like a cop?" She looked over her shoulder briefly. It made him think that she really was hiding something illegal in her car. He'd seen that nervous expression many times on many guilty parties.

"Yes, just like a cop, but my jurisdiction is not the

streets. I typically investigate crimes in the national forests and federal land."

She leaned back in her seat. Had he just seen her sigh in relief? The expression only escalated his senses. Tru's little sister wasn't as innocent as he liked to think. But the idea of telling Tru this only exacerbated Bard's guilt from the last time he told his friend someone he cared about couldn't be trusted.

Bard folded his arms, his gun pressed against his forearm. "I can still make arrests when I see a crime being committed."

Her eyes widened for a moment before she dropped her gaze to her hands in her lap.

He returned the gun to the holster at his back. "I'm going to tend to my dog for a moment. Then I want you to follow me to my office so we can have a real talk. I'll fill you in on everything that went down with your brother. You're going to need to know the details so you can be safe. And that goes for the rest of your family too."

Bard stood still for a moment as he watched Luci bite her lower lip. When she faced forward, he stepped back and let her close the door. She looked so childlike behind the driver's seat even though he knew she was about twenty-six. *Can she even see over the steering wheel?* he wondered as he turned and took three steps toward his car.

On his fourth step, she took off.

Bard whipped around; his mouth dropped in shock. He was having a hard time separating Luci Butler from the fact that only criminals ran. Tru's sister's guilt was as blatant as his own.

He raced around the front of the car and jumped in behind the wheel. As her taillights disappeared into the darkness, his gut instinct told him to cuff her and take her in.

No, he fought against the thought. *That's not why I came here.*

Bard was trying to turn over a new leaf when it came to judging suspects. After ten years of investigations, he'd been burned enough times when he had given people the benefit of the doubt. What took ten years to form in him would not come undone in a matter of weeks.

"God, help me to see between black and white. Where is the gray in Luci Butler's situation? Because from where I stand, she is up to something, and it's not good."

Bard took the next turn as she led him into Old Santa Fe—the downtown from long before the Plaza was established and claimed the title. He scanned the side streets of old stucco buildings for anyone lurking and lying in wait. The gunman couldn't have gone far. Bard could only pray the guy wasn't waiting for Luci at her place. She could be racing straight into danger.

He picked up his speed to catch up as Hero gave a woof from the back seat.

"Yeah, she's in a hurry all right. I'm pretty sure she's trying to lose me." He sighed and shook his head as Luci's innocence dissipated with each turn. "But regardless of guilt, I won't let anything bad happen to her…if I can catch the little spitfire, that is."

Without talking to her brother, Luci had no plans to trust this investigator guy—if his title was even true. She took the back street behind her building, a two-story adobe structure, and pulled into an unlit parking spot. She usually parked out front where the streetlights didn't allow for the lurking shadows of muggers, but tonight she needed the cover.

Luci shut her car door and opened the back for the painting. After all the delays that night, she now only had three hours to take the painting out of the frame, add the missing touches, let it dry and reframe it. Then of course, return it to the gallery with Sal being none the wiser.

But would the buyer notice the subtle differences?

She hit the stairs that led to her studio on the second floor.

A clicking sound stopped her halfway up. Luci froze and turned around, but the darkness revealed no sign of anyone.

Then the bouncing headlights of the towering giant filled the scene before her. She stepped back into the shadows of the stairway, hoping he hadn't seen her. She also took notice of her surroundings. By the square trash bins, something moved but quickly disappeared.

An animal?

The man who pointed the gun at her and demanded the painting?

Luci turned quickly and ran up the rest of the way, hoping Bard hadn't seen her. From the balcony, she saw him drive to the corner and take a right, away from her building.

"Phew," she sighed in relief. He hadn't seen her.

With time ticking down, she punched her code into the security box by the door and rushed inside, closing it tight behind her and dead-bolting it. The worn vestibule between the exterior door and her studio door had one dim light bulb to guide her. Using her key, she let herself in and locked the studio door behind her. Her first attempt at losing Bard had failed. He followed her to the building. She could only hope he didn't know she lived up here. Being that these second-floor studio units above the storefronts weren't deemed residential, she hoped he would keep on driving to look for real apartments that people lived in. People who weren't starving artists who settled for a couch in their workspace.

Luci tripped over some drop cloths as she dashed to place the painting on the easel.

A bang on the exterior door stopped her in mid-movement.

He hadn't kept driving.

"I know you're in there, Luci. I just need to talk to you and fill you in. Then I will go." His voice sounded muffled with the two doors between them.

She leaned the painting on the floor against the legs of the easel and opened her studio's door to respond. "Go away. This isn't a good time." She glanced back at the painting of the lady in red. Her eyes were wrong. All wrong. "I have work to do, and I don't have much time to do it. Can we talk in the morning?"

"It is the morning. Three a.m. exactly. This can't wait. You've already had a gun on you once tonight. Don't you want to know why?"

I need to paint. It was all that mattered to her right now.

"Listen, I could be in a lot of trouble if I don't get this project done tonight. Come back after eight. We'll talk then. Plus, I want to hear from my brother before I let you in. How do I know you really know him?"

"He's in love with a woman named Danika. In the years I've known him at the park, I've never seen him so happy."

Luci dropped the side of her head against the door she held. She felt a soft smile of peace and gratefulness twitch on her face. "I haven't met her yet. Is she nice? Is she good for him?"

"Yes, but…"

Luci lifted her head in quick concern for Tru. "But? What's wrong with her?"

"Nothing. It's part of the reason why I'm here. What I have to tell you."

Luci squeezed her eyes and frowned at what she knew she would do. If only Tru had called her back to confirm he knew Bard, she would have felt better about letting him into her workspace. A glance at the pillow on the tattered couch and throw blanket spilling onto the floor reminded her she was also crashing here.

Then her gaze fell to the woman in the painting…and she frowned.

Her eyes were wrong. Those weren't her eyes. These eyes didn't hold her knowledge.

"This better be quick," Luci said and took the two steps into the vestibule, closing her studio door behind her. She turned the dead bolt, and Bard rushed in quick and smooth and closed the door all in one moment.

He also had his dog. Luci was glad to see him not barking anymore.

Bard turned the lock and faced her; his tall muscular frame filled the space so much that her breath caught, and she backed into the door to her studio. There wasn't enough space in here for the three of them.

"What kind of dog is he?" she asked warily, never one to feel comfortable around big dogs.

Or their big owners.

"Belgian Malinois. Can we go inside?" Bard asked, nodding to the door to her studio.

"Why can't you speak here?" Luci tried to swallow past her drying throat. His nearness made her feel so much smaller than her four-foot-eleven-inch height.

"I suppose I could, but you have to admit, there's not much space in here. I feel like I'm crowding you. Plus, I'd like to check your place out to be sure nothing's been tampered with. Make sure our friend with the gun hasn't already been here."

Luci sighed in disappointment at herself. Why hadn't she thought of that? She had just barged in without giving a thought to the fact that her place may have been occupied. "It's only one room, but I suppose there's plenty of places to hide behind." She was caving. *Why?* Because she felt like a child with this man? He was tall and muscular, but he wasn't necessarily overly domineering. The only time he'd barked at her was when he told her to stop at the gallery. "Fine, you can come in."

Luci reached behind her and turned the doorknob. As soon as she opened the door, Hero let out a deep woof.

In the next second, before either of them could stop the dog, Hero charged past her, making a direct line for the *Lady in Red*.

"No!" Luci shouted as she dived to stop him from attacking the framed painting.

Her fingers reached far…but not far enough.

The loud crack of glass echoed through the fifteen-by-fifteen room as Hero slammed into the painting head-on, knocking it to the ground. He sat proudly beside the frame, his tongue hanging out the side of his mouth as he panted. His pointy ears perked straight to the ceiling, and he seemed pleased with himself.

Luci looked from the dog to its owner. The man's eyes filled with accusation, and he directed it right at her. "Luci, do you have something you want to tell me?"

THREE

"If you don't open that painting up, I will." Bard took his keys from his pocket and snapped open a small pocketknife linked to the ring.

"No!" Luci stepped between him and the painting on the floor. "Okay, just let me do it. You could ruin it, if your dog hasn't already. Would you remove him from it, please?"

Bard put his keys back and called Hero to his side. "Good boy." Bard patted his head.

"Good boy?" Luci knelt beside the frame with its spiderweb cracks covering what appeared to be a woman in a red dress. "I wouldn't call what he did good. Do you have any idea how much frames cost? Does it look like I can afford to replace it? And the painting inside is unique and one of a kind." She lifted the frame gently and turned it over. The fall of broken glass cascaded to the wood floor and caused her to pause and close her eyes.

Bard took in the thin body kneeling beside the solid wooden frame. "I take it you spend more money on them than you do on food."

"My work is my bread and butter. If I don't sell my art, I don't eat. A good frame can help display the art in a more appealing way. Sometimes the frame is part of the piece." She gazed up at him, and the light bulbs caught her long, sweeping lashes above her heated eyes.

Truman's sister was stunning.

Bard cleared his throat as his train of thought caught him off guard. Then he noticed her lashes glistened with unshed tears and he stepped away uncomfortably. He needed to focus on what he had come for, and it wasn't to arrest her for drugs, whether she was guilty of trafficking or not. "Luci, if you're in trouble, I can help you. I came to be sure you're safe, but that doesn't just mean from some outside criminal." He scanned the room full of painting supplies and an old couch with obvious evidence that she also lived here. It wasn't much in the way of a home. "I know sometimes life can be tough, and decisions that are made in the moment may not always be very wise."

"I am not selling anything but paintings. I'll show you," she said, her thin lips pursed in annoyance. Then she cut into the backing of the frame. She reached her slender fingers inside and tore the brown paper away with a gasp.

Three bricks of a white substance were taped to the back of the canvas. Cocaine, if Bard was to guess.

"I didn't put those there." She glanced up with eyes so wide and filled with genuine terror. "Honest. Those weren't there when I framed this." Her head shook back and forth repeatedly. "Please, you have to believe me."

Bard felt he'd hit a crossroads. In an ordinary takedown, he would arrest the suspect and let the courts deal with them. It was his job to provide the evidence to convict. That was all.

He had seen Luci Butler steal this painting, and now, she had drugs in her possession. He had plenty of evidence to put her away for a very long time.

"Here, just take them," she said and reached for them.

"Don't touch!" he ordered, stopping her before her fingers made contact on the plastic.

Had he just made up his mind about her? She looked guilty, but he didn't want to go on looks. That's what got him into trouble with Tru and the woman he loved.

"You could leave fingerprints behind," he explained for his outburst. He sighed and pinched the bridge of his nose, trying to figure out what to do in this situation. "How many other paintings have you sold through this gallery?"

Luci stood and went to the couch to perch on the end. She looked even smaller with her shoulders hunched and the look of fear on her face. She bit her lower lip and folded her hands in a tight grip on her knees. "About ten."

"In how long?"

"Three months, maybe almost four."

"And you didn't think it odd that your paintings were suddenly selling so fast?"

Her teeth let go of her lower lip, and she curled it his way. "What does that mean? That my work isn't good?"

"That's not what I said. I just mean the bricks of cocaine would explain why the paintings were jumping off the wall. It appears Salazar Art Gallery is a front for drug trafficking. And whether you knew this or not, your name is scrawled across the bottom of that painting. I'd say if you're as innocent as you claim to be, then you're being set up to take the fall."

* * *

"Who is Salazar?" Bard asked after carefully moving the bricks to under one of the easels with his foot. "And how long have you known him?"

"Sal is my friend," Luci responded as she stood in front of the woman in the painting. Now that the canvas was no longer encased in the frame, Luci studied her eyes and mixed oil paint colors on a palette to get the correct earthy green to be accurate.

"That's not what I asked," Bard said. "Who is he?"

"Well, that's all you're going to get from me. Sal took a chance on me when no one else would. I won't be involved in a ploy to make him a guilty man."

"He's only guilty if he's actually smuggling drugs. Which means you'd be protecting a drug trafficker. What's the crime rate in this area?"

She shrugged, uncertain and swiped her first stroke on the painting. She tilted her head and closed her eyes for a moment. When she opened them again, the tip of her brush moved fast and bold to match the image in her mind.

"Who is she?" Bard asked, stepping beside her.

Luci knew he was referencing the woman in the painting. "I don't know," she replied. "She sits in the Plaza every afternoon selling her turquoise. I didn't get her eyes right. I went by her yesterday and realized my mistake. I had to fix it. I couldn't let her go until I did."

"Even if it meant you were caught and arrested?"

She tore her gaze from the painting to focus on him. "I had to fix her."

He sighed and crossed his arms in front of his chest. "What about her eyes isn't right? And why does it matter?"

Luci shook her head at such an ignorant thing to say. "Are you always this uncouth?"

"If you mean to the point, then yes. Just answer the question."

Luci focused on the intense message in the woman's eyes. "She knows something. I don't know what, but there are so many answers hidden in her gaze."

"Hmm…and you say she sits in the Plaza selling gems?"

"Turquoise is not a gem. It's a stone. She makes jewelry from her pieces, and they are lovely, but…"

"But what?"

She frowned. "Nobody really buys them. They pass her by for the high-end stores."

"Still, is she always in the Plaza?" he asked.

Luci nodded. "If she didn't show, she could lose her spot to another artist. As beautiful as her jewelry is, her clothes are worn. She needs to be there." Luci pointed her brush toward a place where the woman's red dress was tattered.

"Then she might know who's been coming and going at the gallery. I'm going to need to talk to her."

"People come and go all day long. Santa Fe is filled with tourists year round. I doubt she's been memorizing the gallery's patrons."

"Then what does she know?"

Luci sighed and locked her gaze on the woman's. "I wish I knew."

"Okay then, tell me about Sal."

She sighed in frustration. "There's nothing to tell. You're like your dog and barking up the wrong tree. Maybe investigating is the wrong business for you." She couldn't stop the dig from springing from her lips. After his offhand comment about her paintings not being good enough to sell quickly, she couldn't help herself.

Bard patted his dog's head. "Don't listen to her. You're a good boy, and you got it right. There'll be big, tasty treats when you get home."

The dog's ears perked again while his round black eyes shined.

Luci painted on. If the man noticed her insult, he ignored it.

"You give me no choice but to turn you into the authorities, Luci."

All right, maybe he did notice.

"I did nothing wrong." She continued to focus on the woman's eyes.

"The drugs in your possession say otherwise. The theft I watched tonight does as well."

"I wasn't stealing it. I was only borrowing it until the buyer could pick it up."

"And who's the buyer?"

"How am I supposed to know? Someone who walked in and liked it enough to put money down. I don't ask for names. It's none of my business."

"Well, it *is* Sal's business, so he would know. Can you get into his computer?"

"Sal is old-school. It's paper and pen for him only. He doesn't even own a computer. Jemez, on the other hand, does. He's been trying to get Sal to step into the present day."

"Jemez?"

"Cody Jemez, but sometimes he just goes by Jemez. He's Sal's most recent hire. He's been manning the gallery. As Sal's wife is ill. Cancer." Luci frowned thinking about sweet Natalie.

"A new hire. A sick wife. So much motive and convenience for opening the doors to crime."

"Or increasing business." She tore her gaze from the canvas to eye Bard. "Are you always this cynical?"

"It's called intuitive where I come from. Part of the job." Now Bard frowned. "Although, I really am trying to withhold my quick judgment. I hurt a friend with my hasty assumptions. Your brother, actually. I misjudged Danika, and I regret it."

"Danika?" Luci went back to the painting.

"Yes. I believed the worst of her. But for now, I would appreciate if you would just tell me what you know of Cody Jemez."

Hero let out a soft whine. Bard put his hand on the dog's head.

Luci continued to paint without deeming an answer to him.

Hero whined again. Bard glanced down at his dog. "Something wrong, buddy?"

Hero swiped his front paw over his snout quickly. Then a shout from somewhere outside led him to the only window.

Bard stepped back and raced to the exit. "We have to go, Luci."

He said something else, but she barely heard him as she was lost in her work. Until he grabbed the brush from her hand.

"Hey!" It felt as though she was being pulled down a vortex as she withdrew from the creative state of her mind.

"Did you not hear me? I said the building is on fire. We have to go. With all these paints and thinners, this place is bound to blow."

"Blow?" Luci looked around her studio—the only home she had. She may have had meager belongings, but what she did have meant everything to her. "I can't go anywhere without my things."

"Like what?"

"Like my photo albums from my childhood. When… when my family was whole."

"What good is any of it if you're dead? Forget it. We have to go. Now."

Luci dropped her brush and ran to a closet for another box. As she turned back, flames flicked at the window and smoke billowed up from the floor. Bard was right about the explosive materials in the studio. She knew she was being childish in wanting her personal things, but no matter how much she tried to reason with herself, she couldn't make the move to run out the door.

She looked to Bard, holding it wide for her. "Please. I can't lose my life again," she pleaded, knowing she wasn't making sense if she was willing to die in a fire. "Help me."

He glanced at the window in indecision. "Luci, your life is at risk." But even as he said it, he rushed toward her and pulled down the albums and knickknacks on display, tossing them all in the box. There wasn't much from her life in this small room, but they managed to get it all. Then he scooped that box up and pushed her through the choking smoke billowing around them. As he led the way to the door, Luci sidestepped and lifted the painting from the easel. She couldn't leave the woman behind either. For one, it was sold. And for two, it felt wrong to let her burn.

"What about the cocaine?" Bard shouted over the increasing roaring fire.

"What about it? I don't want it."

Bard's eyes widened, but he quickly bent down and picked up the bricks with a clean rag from the easel, dropping them into her box of things. They exited and ran down the stairs and out to the parking lot.

Then Bard halted and shouted for her to get down. He dropped the box and stepped in front of her.

"What's going on?" she asked, tilting her head back to stare up over his large back. She held the canvas at her side.

"You have a flat tire."

"Flat?" She tried to see around him, but his giant form wouldn't let her. Did she even come up to his neck? "It wasn't flat before."

He scanned the area to her left and right before turning around. He stepped close and wrapped his arms around her like a cocoon. "You don't have one flat. You have four. They've been slashed." He pushed her back into the shadows, even as the flames flicked close to her back. "And whoever slashed your tires also started the fire. Whether you want to admit it or not, you're in big trouble, Luci. Dangerous and deadly trouble."

FOUR

Bard had one focus in mind: get Luci to the safety of his car. Upon arriving at her studio, he had parked around the corner in the shadows. To get there now, he had to guide her close to the burning building. He instructed Hero to stand behind her as he took the lead right in front of her with the box of her measly belongings under one arm and his gun in his other hand.

As Bard made his way to the corner, he scanned the area in the light. A streetlamp gave some direction, while the fire caused flickering shadows before him. He could see his car tucked in by the tree line, and from here, it appeared his tires were fine.

"Let's go," he said under his breath and picked up his pace to cross the parking lot to his car. As soon as he reached the passenger side, he opened the front door for Luci and the back door for Hero, tossing the box inside after him. The three white bricks of cocaine sat at the top, and as he shut the door, sirens filled the air. Firefighters and police were on the way, and he knew he should turn her over to them.

But she had been willing to leave the drugs behind in the fire.

Bard couldn't shake that fact. If she was guilty of smuggling cocaine, she would know the ramifications of showing up to the buyer empty-handed. Luci hadn't cared about retrieving them. What she cared about was her photo albums. Before he could decide on what to do with her, he caught a movement on the side of the building.

In the next moment, the front passenger door flung wide just as a gunshot rang out, its impact hitting the door. Luci had opened the door just in time to give him a shield of protection.

"Get in!" she yelled as she climbed behind the wheel. "Give me the keys." When he hesitated, she said, "Now!"

Bard had no choice but to toss her the keys and let her drive. The alternative of staying behind to wait for the police wasn't an option. For the time being, his decision of what to do with her was put on hold. She had the car in gear and screeching out of the parking lot before he even shut the door.

Another round of gunshots hit the car and smashed something out behind them, most likely the rear light. She took the right turn out of the parking lot practically on two wheels, and it wasn't until they were a mile down the road that he realized she was heading in the opposite direction that the sirens had been coming from.

Coincidence? Or had Luci just saved her own hide?

"You seem like you've driven a getaway car before," he said, not sure if he wanted to hear her response. Everything within him screamed to turn her over to the police. He'd caught her stealing. He'd caught her with cocaine in her possession. In his black-and-white world, she was guilty. Aiding and abetting her made him guilty as well. "I hope I'm not throwing away a ten-year-long career, not to mention having to do time."

She looked in the rearview mirror and her side mirrors. "This is my first getaway. But it's also my first time being shot at. There's just something about that sound, I guess. Especially twice in one night." She accelerated the car. "And for the hundredth time, those are *not* my drugs."

Bard kept watch in his side mirror but also cast glances Luci's way. She looked so small behind the wheel. "I'm surprised you can reach the pedals."

She sent him a quick scathing look. "This coming from a behemoth. I'm surprised you can even fit in the door. Where are we going anyway?"

He bit back a smirk. "Can you break back into your gallery?"

She shrugged her slender shoulder. "Sure. I have to return the painting anyway. But why do you want to go there?"

"Because if you're innocent like you say you are, then the real drug smuggler is the gallery owner. I want Hero to have a sniff around."

Luci pulled over in an instant and stopped the car.

"What's wrong?" he hollered, looking around the dark streets. Not another car was around. "Why did you do that?" he demanded, checking on Hero in the back seat.

"I won't take you to Salazar Art Gallery if all you plan to do is look for a way to incriminate Sal. He is my friend." Her piercing green eyes in the lights from the dashboard bore into him with determination to protect the gallery owner.

"Even if that means I turn you in, instead? Are you

willing to go to jail for this guy? What exactly has he done for you?"

"He has been there for me, supporting me and my work. He has been more of a parent to me than my own birth parents. I won't set him up."

"Luci, the man set *you* up."

"You don't know that."

"I *will* know as soon as we get inside the gallery. You owe it to yourself to find out."

"I owe Sal more." Her slender chin lifted defiantly.

"Financially?" Bard wondered if Sal needed to push drugs through her paintings to compensate any funds he had sent Luci's way.

"No, I have earned every penny he has given me. That's the point. It's because he has pushed my paintings that I am finally making an income to at least pay the studio rent and buy some food."

Bard cast a glance at her bony wrist. "Not enough," he muttered under his breath. "But, okay, fine. I won't turn him in." *Yet.* "I just want to look around. Perhaps I will find a clue of who the guy is that has tried to kill you four times tonight, in case you weren't counting."

Her lips trembled into a frown, and on a sigh, she pulled back onto the road.

"I'm glad you're finally seeing reason. It's not normal to take the fall for something like this," he said in relief.

"I don't know what normal is. I once thought I did, but then I learned that life can change in the blink of an eye. One second, you're planning what you're going to wear for the school dance, and the next, you're an outcast. Normal is a facade." She drove on without an explanation.

Bard knew a bit about the Butler family's circumstances. He knew the oldest sibling had suffered amnesia from a car accident about twelve years ago, and only recently regained his memories. "Tru had told me a bit about your brother, Jett. Is that what you mean by life changing quickly?"

"It's only part of it. But yeah, it definitely was the catalyst to everything else." The way she said *everything else* made him wonder what those things might be. They didn't sound pleasant.

They were also none of his business, he told himself. He needed to stay focused on protecting her and figuring out who was after her. And who planted the drugs in her painting.

Bard turned back to Hero. The dog kept his gaze locked on the white bricks, sending quick glances his way as if to say, "Are you seeing this?"

"Good boy," he told his trusted companion.

Luci looked in her rearview mirror and huffed. "He's aggressive. And big." She eyed Bard. "Sort of like you."

"He's smarter than me." Bard smirked.

"It takes maturity to admit that." She flashed a quick smile his way, and for one moment, Luci's true beauty shined through her whimsical eyes and stole his breath from his lungs.

It took Bard a few concentrated breaths before he could speak again. He kept his face toward the passenger window and caught his startled reflection staring back at him in the glass. Once he regained his composure, he stole a glimpse of her profile as she drove back to Old Santa Fe, and suddenly felt like the worst friend in the world.

Bard had come here to mend the broken fence with Tru by protecting Luci from possible danger. Seeing her as anything other than his little sister would be the destruction of another fence and a line he couldn't cross.

"You're awfully quiet all of a sudden." She sent raised inquisitive eyebrows his way. *And those lashes!* "Is something wrong?"

"Yes, I mean no," he muttered quickly.

Her eyes danced in the light so becomingly, and Bard knew he could be out a friend if he wasn't careful.

"Well, which is it?" she asked. "Do I have reason to be concerned?"

"I won't lie to you, Luci. You have every reason to be concerned, and you should be very afraid." Bard vowed not to bring more disruption to her life than she'd already lived through and had to face with this killer now on her heels. Even if that meant he got used to having no air in his lungs when she looked his way.

Luci drove down the dark streets of Old Santa Fe, passing the adobe buildings of businesses and residences. The streetlights cast a golden hue on the area, but they also allowed for places to hide in the shadows. She moved Bard's car slowly down the back alley behind the gallery, parking it by the rear exit. They sat still for a moment, scanning the area, particularly down by the dumpster. She noticed Bard hadn't said a word in a while. He'd said nothing was wrong, so perhaps he was just a quiet person. The truth was she didn't know him at all.

"I don't take you for a brooding man, so your silence has me worried," she said. "What are you keeping from me?"

"I have kept nothing from you since we met. If anything, I'm the one in the dark. I'm breaking a lot of laws tonight to give you the benefit of the doubt." Bard looked at the door. "I can't promise you that I'll continue to break laws once we go through that door. Luci, I am a by-the-book cop, so I need you to cut me some slack here. Nothing I've done tonight is how I would typically respond. But after letting your brother down by not believing in the woman he loves, I'm making every effort not to repeat that mishap with you."

She tilted her head. "What exactly did you do that you feel so guilty about? To the point that you would seek me out to protect me?"

Bard's jaw ticked as his eyes closed for a moment. On a sigh, he said, "Tru is my friend. Or rather, he was. At a moment when I should have been there for him and listened more carefully to him, I wasn't and didn't. He had smugglers at Carlsbad National Park and was responsible for keeping people safe. Danika came to help, and instead of trusting her, I made Tru doubt her. I made him think the worst about her because I thought the worst of her. I considered her guilty before innocent. Because of that, I lost a friend."

Luci huffed and pursed her lips. At least she knew where she stood with this man. "So you're saying you haven't turned me in because of who my brother is, and not because you believe me to be innocent?"

"Luci, I watched you steal that painting off the wall. I watched you remove the canvas from the frame. For all I know, you were about to remove the drugs and your excuse of fixing her eyes was just that—an excuse. If you were anyone else, I would've already put the cuffs on you and let a judge decide if you were telling the truth or not."

She looked to his waist. "You have cuffs on you?"

The man wore tan tactical pants and a black polo under a leather coat. Somewhere in there he carried his gun. She hadn't thought about handcuffs.

He reached behind him, and in the next second, he held a pair of metal handcuffs. They swung there between them, and she knew by all pretenses, she looked guilty. The idea of him putting them on her made her feel like she'd hit rock bottom.

Instant tears clouded her vision. She squeezed her eyes to push them away and lifted her chin with more bravado than she felt. "I don't know if this means anything to you or not, but I appreciate you not taking me in. I know it doesn't mean that you actually believe in me, but if you don't mind, I'd like you to let me think that you do. Even if it's a lie." She didn't know how to explain to him that she didn't have anyone to believe in her.

Only Sal.

Hero huffed in the back seat and drew his owner's attention to him. Bard looked at his dog and then at her. He nodded once. He didn't look happy about giving her the benefit of the doubt, and she knew he had a lot on the line, most likely his badge.

The man shifted in his seat to lean closer to her, the look in his eyes intense. "I need to know that you'll let me do my job, even if it means I find something out that incriminates your friend."

"You won't," she said quickly.

"Are you saying that because he believed in you or because you know the truth?"

"I'm saying that because I believe in him," she replied.

Bard leaned back on a sigh. He looked back at the door and pressed his lips tight, flinging the car door open. "Let's go in and find out if your belief in him is warranted, or not."

Luci hesitated to follow, but he still dangled the handcuffs. She had no choice. She opened her door and hoped her trust in Sal wasn't misplaced.

"My keys are in the box with my things," she said, eyeing the large dog guarding the box with his life.

Bard opened the back door and whistled for Hero to get out. He then reached in for the box.

Luci opened the other side door and grabbed her painting. She was careful to hold the edges of the canvas as she walked around the front of the car and met Bard at the gallery door. She gently placed the canvas up against the wall.

"What do you plan to do with that?" he whispered as she reached for the keys in the box.

Unlocking the door, she pushed it and grabbed the painting. "I'm going to put it back."

"You don't really think the buyer is coming for it, do you? It wasn't the painting they wanted."

Luci held the door for him as he entered with Hero, then closed it behind him and locked it. "You don't know that. Perhaps the buyer has nothing to do with this."

With only the limited streetlights shining through the storefront windows, Bard's face remained in the dark shadows, but she could tell he waited for her to face the facts.

No one was buying her paintings for their excellence.

"Do you always call things like you see them, even if it's cruel?" she asked and moved past him with the painting. She entered the office and flipped through a rack of other paintings. Checking to be sure the lady's eyes were dry, Luci inserted her canvas in the middle and flipped the others back over it. She would let Sal know where to find it for the buyer…*if* there really was a buyer. She supposed Bard was right, but she held out hope that someone out there wanted her work.

"Sometimes the truth hurts," he said, stepping toward the desk and turning on his phone flashlight. He illuminated the surface of the desk and all the papers strewn upon it.

"Gee, thanks. You also know how to kick someone when they're down."

He glanced her way, realization dawning on his face. "I didn't mean it to come out like that. There's nothing wrong with your painting. It's pretty."

"I wasn't really going for pretty, but fine." Luci shook her head in annoyance. The sooner she could get rid of the cynical Bard and his overbearing dog, the sooner she could figure out who was behind setting her up.

He picked up some papers to read in the phone light. "What were you going for?"

She walked over to the filing cabinet and found it locked. She moved over to the desk to grab a paperclip and unwound it. "Reassurance, maybe." She thought of the lady in red who sat at the corner selling her wares each day. "Wisdom," she said and inserted the thin piece of metal into the keylock carefully, feeling for the release of the mechanism inside. A quick click and she pulled the door wide.

Turning back to Bard, she caught him watching her with pressed lips. "You do realize when I see you do things like this, it only makes you look guiltier. Where did you learn to pick a lock?"

Luci shrugged, thinking back to her first time. "High school. Mr. Gaffney's candy bar stash." She watched

Bard's eyes widen. "Don't worry. I left money. I've never stolen anything in my life."

He scoffed and flung a hand to reference the rack of paintings.

"What? It's back. Sort of."

The way Bard let out a deep breath told her his patience was wearing thin. She thought of the handcuffs and pulled the drawer wider. "This is where all the receipts are for the gallery sales."

"All of them?" Bard stepped closer to peer inside. "It looks like there's enough here to go back years. This could take days. We don't have days. I figure we have about ten minutes before our guy shows up. If that. We'll have to take it all with us." He turned to look for something to put the receipts into and grabbed a shopping bag from underneath the counter.

Hero whined from the office corner.

Bard said, "Fill this up with those. I'm going to check out the gallery to see what's got him upset. The fact that he's not alerting me to more drugs, tells me your painting was the only one stuffed. But something's up."

He left with his dog beside him, and Luci dug deep into the drawer to scoop up handfuls of receipts. When she had every last slip of paper in the bag, she closed the cabinet and stepped out of the office.

In that moment, the glass of the storefront shattered inward as gunshots rang out one after another, spraying bullet holes throughout the gallery and destroying many pieces of work around her.

"Get down!" She heard Bard's voice shout somewhere in the gallery. Suddenly, she felt a hand squeeze her forearm and yank her to the floor. She landed on his hard chest, and he quickly rolled her over and shielded her from the unrelenting bullets flying by.

"Looks like your friend is back," he said through gritted teeth near her ear. The constant discharge of ammo told her this was not a handgun like before. "And this time, he's not leaving until the job is done."

FIVE

This guy was out for blood. As Bard hovered over Luci to shield her from the onslaught of flying bullets, he expected at any second to take one somewhere in his body. The viciousness of the shoot-up told him that this was more than someone wanting a few bricks of cocaine. This was personal. Whoever this man was wanted Luci dead.

But why?

Bard opened his eyes and stared straight into hers, wide with fright. He wanted to believe in her innocence, but the extent this shooter had gone through this evening only told Bard that Luci was a liability. Was it more than her involvement in smuggling drugs? Did she know something that this man wanted to keep secret? Or was this a vendetta playing out before his eyes?

The shooting stopped and a strange silence filled the atmosphere. A few hanging pieces of glass let go and shattered to the floor in the aftermath. Bard knew he had to get her out before he heard footsteps crunching over the destruction.

He shifted away from her and whispered, "Get to the back door. Stay low. I'm right behind you." When she hesitated, he said, "Don't look back. Just go."

Luci rolled over onto her stomach and shimmied her way toward the back door. Thankfully, they hadn't entered the full gallery and there was no glass back in the hall. He followed her with Hero beside him, the dog staying low in his stealth-like crawl. Bard grabbed the bag of receipts on his way and, at the door, whispered, "Stay right there. Do you have the keys to my car?"

With a frantic nod and trembling fingers, she reached into her pants pocket and held up the small key ring with one key on it. The car wasn't his personal vehicle but one he borrowed from the Bureau when he arrived at the Santa Fe office.

"Don't lose it. It's the only one I have."

"What about the box of my things? And the drugs?" she whispered.

Bard seriously wanted to leave them behind and get out of there, but those bricks were evidence. He moved behind her to turn back for the box.

As he heard footsteps crunch on the glass by the storefront door—or what was left of it—he also heard sirens off in the distance, which meant the shooter knew he only had seconds to finish the job.

"On the count of three," Bard whispered close to her ear. "You get to the car. I will get the box. Take Hero with you."

"What about you?"

Bard removed his gun from his side holster. "I've got my friend. One…two…three!"

On three, they each made their move—Luci for the door, Bard for the box by the office door. Their movement set off another string of gunshots, this time from the man's handgun.

But Bard also shot off his weapon in the direction

of the front door. The sound of the shooter crying out in pain told Bard his shot had been true. It gave him an extra moment to reach for the box and exit the back door Luci had left open for him. He jumped into the passenger seat, keeping his gun at the ready as she put the car in reverse and craned her neck over her shoulder to drive backward out of the alley.

The shooter ran out the exit door with his gun aimed at them. Bard rolled down his window and pointed his gun out, taking the first shot. The door splintered by the man's head, and he ducked.

Luci turned the wheel sharply and put the car into Drive as Bard took two more shots out the window. The shooter also managed to take two more that hit the car before she screeched off into the darkness.

It took Bard five minutes before he lowered his weapon to his lap and released his hold on it. "That was close. Too close." He looked back at Hero hunched down low in the back seat, and then he glanced her way. He could see her breathing was shallow. "Are you okay? You weren't hit, were you?"

She shook her head and tried to speak but couldn't. She managed to mouth, "Asthma."

Oh no. She was having an asthma attack? *Now?*

Think, Bard. "Okay, pull over. I'll take over driving. Do you have an inhaler?"

She shook her head. "Fire," she managed to squeak out. He got the picture. It had been left in her studio.

"Do you have another one somewhere?"

She nodded. "Parents'…house. But I…don't want to go…there."

"Luci, I don't think you have a choice. Now pull over."

She did as he asked, and Bard jumped out of his door

to run around to the other side of the car. He helped her from the driver's seat and pulled her close to him, rubbing her back slowly. He pressed his lips to her ear and mimicked slow breathing to try to get her to follow his lead. Gradually, he began to hear her take deeper breaths.

"Don't make me go there," she finally said without gasping for air.

Bard didn't know the history she had with her family other than a few things that her brother had shared with him, but she had a reason, and if it meant risking another asthma attack, he wouldn't force the issue. He guided her over to the other side of the car and helped her inside. Racing back to the driver's seat, he jumped in and had the car in gear again and moving.

With his attention on the road in front of him and behind him, he listened carefully for any hitches in her breathing. She had dropped her head on the headrest and closed her eyes. Reaching over, he brushed the backs of his fingers along her cheekbone. Her head lolled into his hand. She accepted his comfort that he offered. It surprised him to see her trust him in this moment of weakness.

Luci Butler portrayed herself to be a strong and capable young woman, giving the pretense that she didn't need anybody. But there was something about the lack of air that could bring the strongest person to their knees.

Bard searched her face for her normal tan coloring to return. Her lips were still blue, and her complexion was ashen.

"We have to stop for your inhaler. You don't look well."

She reached for his hand at her face and held it there

as she looked over at him. Then she nodded and whispered, "All right," and gave him the address.

Bard hated removing his hand from hers, but he had to input the address into the car's GPS system. Once the computer-generated voice directed him on a twenty-minute drive, he reached back and took her hand that now lay lifeless in her lap. She may not have been wheezing anymore, but her airways were not fully open yet either.

The drive felt like forever. Even Hero sensed the tension in the car and whined from behind them, putting his snout on the back of Luci's seat. When Bard finally pulled up to a small brown stucco home, he wondered if she could walk to the door. But when he came around to help her, she pushed his hands away and managed to get herself up the steps and onto the porch all by herself. However, when she went to knock, she could barely get the door.

Bard took over from there, rapping his knuckles hard against the wood. When the door opened to an older gentleman, Bard saw the resemblance between Tru and his father. Both men had black hair and tan skin, evidence of their indigenous heritage. The man looked with concern at his daughter and opened the door wider to help her inside.

"She needs her inhaler," Bard said.

A short woman, no taller than Luci, came into the room to wrap a robe around her. Instantly, she ran back down the hallway and returned with an inhaler a few minutes later. The woman took Luci, wrapping her arm around her and then bringing her to the couch as Luci inhaled the medicine to open her lungs.

"Who are you?" the man asked Bard.

"I'm Bard Holland, an investigator for the Bureau of Land Management."

At the man's confusion, Bard wondered how much he should share with him. Knowing how Luci hesitated to come here kept him tight-lipped for a few moments. These two people seemed kind enough, but Luci had a reason for not trusting them. He tried to think if Tru ever mentioned anything bad about his parents, but Bard didn't think it was anything more than inconsequential information. That only told him that Tru's family wasn't very close with each other.

"Bard's a friend," Luci removed the inhaler and said quickly.

Bard knew it was just an excuse, but he liked her referring to him as a friend. It felt like a milestone had just been passed. But if she turned out to be guilty, friend or not, he would still take her in.

"A friend who's an investigator?" Mr. Butler crossed his arms at his chest and narrowed his eyes at Bard. The way he stood, Bard knew he had been in the military at some point. "Is there something we should know?"

Bard replied, "Nothing to worry about right now. However, I would suggest keeping the place locked up just in case something should come to your doorstep."

Genuine concern covered Luci's parents' faces. Her mother sat down beside her with worried hands clenched together. "Bard? Is Luci in danger?"

The answer was a blatant yes, but the shake of Luci's head told him to keep things under wraps. "Right now, she's safe. I'm working to figure out who might want to harm her. That's all I can say for now. We only came here because she had an asthma attack and needed her inhaler. We shouldn't stay much longer. For the safety of all."

Luci stood, but her mother grabbed her arm. Mrs. Butler looked up at her and said, "Please be careful. We do care about you, whether you want to believe that or not."

"I will. And thank you. Do as Bard had said and lock up." Luci headed for the door, nodding to him to follow her out.

Her quick departure made for an awkward exit for him, but he put his hand out to Mr. Butler and the man took it and shook.

"Keep us informed?" Mr. Butler asked.

"We'll do our best," Bard said and turned for the door. "Let me exit first," he whispered to her as he passed by. When he stepped to the door, he scanned the streetlights in the neighborhood of similar one-story homes. Daylight was coming over the horizon, and he realized he still had no answer to the night's horrendous events. But a scan of the area told him they hadn't been tracked there. He needed direction and thought of the bag of receipts. With the sun coming up, he would find a place to go through them.

"Go ahead," he told Luci. "It's safe." As Luci stepped outside, he looked back at her parents who now stood beside each other and were probably wondering if they would ever see her alive again. He noticed a painting on the wall behind them. "Is that one of Luci's?" he asked them.

Her mother smiled and nodded. "She's always had a way with the paintbrush. She has a special kind of talent." Mrs. Butler frowned. "We know we failed her and should have been there to be supportive of her in her formative years. Please, Bard, we have so much to make up for..." Her voice trailed off, but he understood what she was saying.

"I'll do my best to make sure you have that opportunity." With that, he pulled the door closed behind him and stepped toward his vehicle, having no foundation to even make such a promise.

"Do you want to talk about it?" Bard asked her as she searched her phone beside him in the car and he drove. She was looking for information about the gallery shooting and found the news broadcast.

"They're calling it a random act of violence," Luci said and showed him the screen. A replay of the reporting by the local news station from the front of Salazar Art Gallery, or what was left of it show on the phone. "It doesn't feel very random to me. It feels personal."

"That's because it is," Bard responded with a frown. "I realized that during the shoot-out. To go to that extent tells me the real reason behind this guy's motives is to see you dead. We just need to figure out why." He took the next turn down a dirt road. "But that's not what I was talking about. I was asking if you wanted to talk about your parents?"

"Where are we going?"

"You're changing the subject."

Luci sighed and put the phone in the cupholder. "And I don't think you're asking."

"Smart girl. What happened between you?"

"Simple. I was forgotten. My parents couldn't handle the stress of losing their oldest son to amnesia, and they couldn't handle a teenager. They could barely stay married. That's all you need to know. Now, where are we going?"

"Away from witnesses."

She eyed him from the corners of her eyes. "Why does that feel just as sinister as this guy tracking me?"

Bard cracked a smile. "Sorry. I just mean I don't want anyone spotting us. I need to go through the receipts, and I don't want any interruptions while I do it."

Luci looked down at the bag. "That could take a while."

"For now, I'm only looking for the ones in the past six months or so. When was the first time you displayed your pieces at the gallery?"

Luci thought of her first painting she sold. "My first sale was at Christmas. Like three weeks before." She smiled at the memory. "I remember being so excited. It had been hanging on the wall since October. I painted a hot-air balloon from the Albuquerque festival. It was a piece that I worked with Sal on. He really helped me fine-tune my craft. It was the first piece that I really knew someone would pay money for. And they did." She looked Bard's way, feeling proud of herself.

"Do you know who bought that piece?" His seriousness perturbed her.

"No. Sal sold it and paid me. He never told me the buyers' names."

"Then what?"

She shrugged. "I don't know. I paid my rent. A lot of good that did. I still ended up losing the place. That's because I took on the rent of the studio. It was foolish of me to think I could handle two rents. But I wanted to be in Santa Fe." She sighed and looked out the window. "And now that place is gone too."

Bard pulled over to a sandy lot with blowing tumble-weeds and cacti dotting the area. "Okay, let's have the bag." He held out his hands, and she lifted it to him. Grabbing a fistful of invoices, he said, "Take out any receipt since September, looking for yours particularly. How many paintings have you sold since that first one at Christmas?"

"Nine large and two small."

"Those are the twelve I'm looking for right now. If I find a pattern, then I'll head in that direction."

The two of them went to work weeding through years of gallery sales. She found the first receipt with her name listed as the painter. Bard found the next one, and within thirty minutes, they had collected all twelve.

And all twelve were the same buyer.

Bard didn't have to tell her that was suspicious. The last four months, her paintings had been selling quickly, and she believed it was because of her talent. So either *Fred Miller* really liked her work, or he liked what was inside it.

"I have to talk to Sal," she said quietly.

Bard restarted the car and put it into gear. "Lead the way. But we need to be careful going there. The shooter could be set up and waiting for us."

Luci gave him the directions to Sal and Natalie's house. Sal had to know by now about his gallery, and she wondered if he'd even be home. But ten minutes later, they pulled up to his house and his car was still in the driveway. Bard carefully led the way, scoping the area out before knocking.

She expected to find the man distraught and prepared herself to comfort him, but when no one answered, she went around the house to find the back kitchen door open. She stepped inside, calling out his name, her voice trailing off as she stepped into a puddle of a dark red liquid.

"Don't go any farther," Bard said in a low tone. "It appears we have another crime scene. And judging by the amount of blood, someone didn't make it."

SIX

Bard had gone through the house and found it empty of any inhabitants—and bodies. The place looked like it had either been ransacked or someone had been in a hurry to pack up and get out. Drawers lay on the floor, pulled from their cabinets with clothes strewn about.

Circling back to the kitchen, he still found Luci standing by the door. She pointed to something across the room. Following her direction, he saw the unmistakable impression of a bullet beside a framed photograph on the wall. Bard touched nothing but speculated that someone had been shot and the bullet had either gone through the person and hit the wall, or this was one bullet that had missed its mark. But apparently not the other one. The smearing on the floor showed someone had been dragged out of here.

But who? Had it been Sal or his wife? Or had Sal shot someone and dragged them out of here? Bard held his tongue on that idea. He knew Luci wouldn't like him saying such a thing about her mentor. Judging by the fact that Sal and his wife's drawers had been rifled through, something told Bard that they were on the run, and dead people don't run.

"We have to call the police," Luci said.

Bard felt his eyes widen at her statement. "I'm glad to hear you say that, but aren't you worried you could be named a suspect. After all, you would have a motive if the man put drugs in your painting and tried to frame you."

She chewed on her lower lip and played with the zipper of her vest. "It's more important that Sal is found. He could be really hurt. Or Natalie. If one of them is bleeding, time is critical. It's obvious they're in danger, and I will do whatever it takes to find them."

Bard retrieved his cell phone from his pocket and dialed the emergency number, telling the dispatcher that he had happened upon a possible crime scene. It would be hard to solve without a body, but the police still needed to come and investigate. This wasn't his jurisdiction, and he needed to let them do their thing. What concerned Bard was Luci's safety. There were too many bullets flying.

"Should we wait in the car?" she asked.

"I would rather you not be seen. But don't touch anything in here. The crime scene unit will have to take prints."

"Will that help them find Sal?" She sounded so little in her worry for her friend. "All of his employees should be notified."

Bard tilted his head at her last comment. "How many employees does he have?"

"Two, plus his wife who helps out at the gallery when she's feeling well enough. But she's more of a decorator in the gallery. Sal acquires the pieces and Natalie displays them. Then he has two people that help him run the place. Delilah Jemez comes in to clean once a week to keep the dust off the artwork, and her son, Cody Jemez, helps in the office. He does some marketing and bookkeeping for Sal. They're both part-time, but the police should look into them and warn them to be safe."

The first cruiser arrived, and Bard met the officer outside. After explaining what they had found so far, he asked Officer Franklin to send a car to the Jemez household to check on them. He then led the man inside as two more officers arrived.

As a team processed the scene, he led Luci into the adjacent living room. This room seemed untouched, and as she stood with her arms folded in front of her, she nodded to a painting on the wall.

"That's one of mine," she said. "We worked on it together this past winter." A soft smile spread on her face, which made him glad to see.

"You obviously care for your friend. If there are any leads here, the police will find him and Natalie. But, Luci, I need to put you someplace safe. You sure you can't stay with your parents?"

Her head shot up as she shook it back and forth. "I'm not ready for that."

"You really don't communicate with your family? Tru never let on about any problems."

"That's because he took off after our brother Jett's accident and went down to Texas. I was left in the house alone to deal with our parents' fighting. I stayed in touch with Tru. In fact, I was planning to have him and Jett over for a picnic in a few weeks. I guess I'll cancel that." She took out her phone and sent off the text to her brothers.

"It's a little early to make that decision, don't you think?"

"I doubt they were going to come anyway. Tru hasn't

even returned my phone call. My brothers are so busy with their lives. They don't have time."

For her. Bard knew that's what she wanted to say. He fought the desire to wrap his arms around her and pull her in for a hug. "Your brother's accident really damaged your whole family. I hadn't realized. When he lost his memory, you all lost something too."

"You could say that again. One day we were a happy family, and the next day everyone fragmented just like Jett's mind. Tru went south to Texas and then to Carlsbad, and my parents nearly divorced."

"And everyone forgot about you."

Luci's eyes shimmered in an instant. He obviously hit a nerve, but she lifted her chin higher toward him, a tough girl to the core. "I can't believe you're getting me to talk about this. I just want to forget everything from that night."

Bard surmised what she wasn't saying. He knew the details of the car crash from when Tru had confided in him. The oldest Butler brother had been set to marry the love of his life. A woman named Nic or Nikki; Bard couldn't remember. But he had been driving late at night when another driver hit and left him for dead. Jett woke up with amnesia and didn't recognize anyone, not even the woman he was to marry. Everyone went their own ways…leaving Luci, the youngest of them all, to fend for herself. Jett may have his memories back, but the family still had a lot of healing to do. And Bard could see why Luci felt forgotten through it all. "That's a lot for a fourteen-year-old to handle."

She shrugged her delicate shoulders. "I got by. And then I met Sal. Suddenly I didn't feel invisible anymore."

"Well, the truth is you're not invisible, but I need

to make you so. So if not your parents' house, where can you go?"

Her cell phone rang. She glanced at the caller ID. "It's Tru."

"See? Your family cares about you. I'll leave you for a few minutes and go check on the police." He turned away, but when he reached the wide doorway into the kitchen, she stopped him.

"Bard," she said, and when he looked over his shoulder, she continued, "I don't know if I've thanked you yet, but thank you. I'm pretty sure I'd be dead already if you hadn't shown up."

Bard frowned, knowing her words were the truth. He made no promises that things wouldn't change for her, though to himself, he vowed to do whatever it took to keep her alive.

Luci turned to face the entertainment center and answered her brother's call. "About time you called me back," she said, trying to sound light and carefree. Instead, she heard anger coming through her voice.

"Sorry, Squirt, we had a missing person in one of the caverns. But he's been found. All is well on this end. It sounds like the same can't be said for you. What's going on? Why is Bard there?"

Luci looked over her shoulder to see the man talking to the officers. He stood with his legs spread apart a bit and his arms folded at his chest. He hovered over the other officers by at least half a foot. But even with his large presence in the small room, he seemed to be genuinely listening to what they were saying.

"He said he came to protect me. He led me to believe you knew about it." Luci tried to remember the man's words from the night before. "He was concerned that someone you upset might retaliate against me. Is that not true?" She hated to think that Bard lied to her. "Is he your friend, or not?"

Tru was silent for a moment. "I once called him a friend, but he led me astray."

"Should I send him packing? Because honestly, Tru, I think I'd be dead if it hadn't been for him last night."

Tru sighed. "I'm not sure, Luci. On the one hand, I'm grateful to him if he has kept you alive, but on the other, I'm still a little upset with him."

"What happened between the two of you?" She lowered her voice so only her brother would hear.

"Let's just say his intuition was wrong, and the wrong person would have gone to jail."

Luci thought of her friend Sal and how Bard seemed to be looking for the evidence to lock him up. "He does seem like the type to fixate on a certain suspect."

"Exactly. While at the same time, the true criminal is getting away." Tru paused. She could tell he was conflicted.

"What should I do? Stick with him or lose him?"

"That's what I'm trying to figure out. I've only known him a few years, but up until this last incident, I would've said don't leave his side. Now I'm not so sure. Who does he think is after you and why?"

"Well, he thought it had something to do with the man from your case. Someone you upset and was still at large."

"Darral Lindsay? Oh man, Luci, I am so sorry. If that's the case, you can't leave Bard's side. Under any circumstances. I didn't even think about Lindsay coming after you, but it makes sense. I just took down his whole operation, and the government has frozen all his assets. He could be out for retaliation, and he wouldn't stop until he took everything away from me as well."

"But what if Bard's going after a friend of mine?"

"Take my advice. Protect your friend at all costs. Bard means well, but even the best law enforcement officers can get it wrong sometimes. Bard was blinded by his past cases."

Luci frowned as she watched Bard discuss the situation with the officers. "He seems good at his job."

"Absolutely. The best."

"And yet, you still doubt him."

"Yeah. I do now. I didn't before, but I could have lost everything dear to me if I had listened to his opinion. He led me to believe Danika was out to hurt me. That she was using me to get into the caves to claim a treasure for herself. If I hadn't come to my senses and realized she could be trusted...well, let's just say we probably wouldn't be alive. It just seems to me that once Bard has determined someone's guilt or innocence, you can't change his mind."

"Yeah, I've noticed." Luci turned back to the entertainment center and caught a small framed picture. It was of her and Sal at his artist cabin. He had taken her out there during the winter. It had been a wonderful retreat and where she had painted the piece on the wall.

She turned back around and looked at the painting they had made together that weekend. It had been a winter scene in the Santa Fe National Forest. She captured the sunrise over the Rio Chama perfectly. Only because he had shared his talents with her. His techniques with the paintbrush changed everything for her. He had been impressed with how quickly she caught on, but it was only because of his tutelage and support. Sal had seen something in her work, but he also had seen *her*.

"I have to protect my friend from Bard," she said quietly.

"He thinks your friend is the one after you?"

Luci huffed with a bit of laughter. "He doesn't understand how important Sal is to me. And vice versa. Sal would never hurt me or set me up for a crime that I didn't commit."

Tru grew quiet again. "I'll admit, I'm a bit conflicted here. I want you safe, but at the same time, I just want you to be aware. And don't be afraid to put Bard on the spot. I wish I had."

Luci closed her eyes at the comfort her brother's words brought her. Of all the people in her family, she was closest to Tru. When everything fell apart in the aftermath of their older brother's accident, the two of them only had each other, even after he left her behind.

"I haven't told you yet, but I'm really happy that you've found where you belong," Luci said. "And with whom you belong."

She could practically hear Tru smile through the phone, and after years of his low outlook on life, and his attempt to isolate himself from everyone, she couldn't be more happy for him.

"I can't wait for you to meet her," he said. "I was a little upset to get your text that you were canceling your picnic in a few weeks. I hope it's just a postponement."

"I'm using the excuse of everything going on, but to be honest, it was probably a dumb thing for me to do anyway. Jett just got his memories back, but he's still keeping his distance. I still have trouble being around Mom and Dad. When everyone wants to see each other, we will. I can't force the family to come back together until everyone is ready. Including myself."

"I don't think it will be much longer, Luce. Jett and Nicole have been building their new home together, and I'm sure we'll all be invited once it's finished."

"And what about your wedding? Do you have a date yet?"

"Not yet, but I promise you you'll be the first to know."

Luci smiled and said goodbye, clicking off just as Bard walked back into the room. Lowering her phone, she looked at the picture of her and Sal.

"I have a safe place to go," she told him. "I won't need you to protect me anymore. No one will find me there."

"And where exactly is there?" Bard's brow furrowed as he stepped closer.

Luci hesitated sharing the location of Sal's remote artist retreat. Tru said he was conflicted about trusting this man, but right now, if she stepped out the front door, she could be shot.

And she didn't have a set of wheels to get to the cabin.

Luci picked up the picture frame and turned it to show Bard. "This is Sal and me at his cabin along the Rio Chama in the Santa Fe National Forest. If you can get me there, you can leave me. There's no road in or out. The only way to get to it is by river raft. He and his wife took me there this past winter. I know I could find it again."

He walked closer and took the picture from her to study it. She could see him sizing Sal up in a two-dimensional photo. But the picture didn't show the larger-than-life man who had so much wisdom to offer. Luci tried to control her resentment for his judgmental opinion of her friend.

Bard looked up over the photo. "The two of you are close." He pressed his lips tight, and she knew he wanted to say more. She dared him with the tilt of her head. He put the picture back onto the shelf. "If his cabin is on national forest property, then I can get the ranger district involved. You know the coordinates of the cabin? I can send someone out there. Perhaps that's where he's hiding out."

"Hiding out?" Luci crossed her arms in front of her. "I don't know the coordinates, and even if I did, I wouldn't tell you. For all I know, you would be sending someone out there to arrest him."

"Only if he's guilty."

More than anything, Luci wanted to leave Bard behind. "Which he's not. I don't think I need your help anymore."

Bard sighed. "Luci, are you sure you can really trust this man? Sometimes people do things that we least expect. Sal could have shot the shooter and dragged out his body."

Before she could respond, one of the officers stepped into the room. "Excuse me, I've just been informed that Cody Jemez has been found dead in his home."

Luci inhaled sharply, covering her mouth. "What happened?"

"He was shot twice in the back, but it doesn't appear that the homicide occurred on his property. The man was moved." The officer stepped out from the room, and Bard looked at her with wide eyes.

"See?"

She could tell this information only made Sal look more guilty. "Things are not always as they seem," she said, but she had to question if she was trying to convince herself of that as well.

SEVEN

Bard knew if Luci had her way, she would lose him as soon as he took his eyes off her. As he pulled into his apartment complex parking lot, he realized she hadn't said much since they left Sal's house. She was probably planning her escape. Except when he looked over at her, he saw she was sound asleep. He parked his car and considered letting her sleep. They could both use a few hours to catch up on their all-nighter. But if they waited any longer, they would lose daylight, and he wasn't up for traipsing through the Santa Fe National Forest in the dark.

Bard reached over and jostled her shoulder. She came awake with a start. "We'll pack up my truck and take that instead of the Bureau's vehicle. We're going to need a raft and supplies. I've already called ahead to the Coyote Forest Ranger's office. They'll have everything ready for us when we get there."

Her long lashes fluttered on her smooth cheeks, and a soft puff of air escaped her lips. Bard wasn't sure if she even understood a word he'd just said to her.

"I know you're tired. It's been a long night for both

of us, but the longer you stay out here, the bigger the target on your back grows."

She nodded and took a deep breath. Letting it out slowly, she said, "I was having a bad dream."

"It wasn't a dream," he said. "This is all really happening."

"But why?" She reached up and pushed her black hair back away from her forehead. "I keep thinking about all that blood. What if…what if they got to Sal too?"

Bard held his tongue about whose blood he believed had been spilled. She knew how he felt and voicing his opinion further would only cause a bigger wedge between them. She may trust Sal, but he was the gallery owner, and Bard found it difficult to believe Sal didn't know drugs were being smuggled through his business. Bard was working extra hard to not convict the man without ever having met him, but with all the evidence, it seemed cut and dried to him.

And that's what got him into trouble the last time.

"There's no sense in worrying about your friend," he said instead, gritting his teeth to stop himself from saying what was really on his mind. "We need to focus on getting you to a safe place, but also getting there safely. The Rio Chama is a major tributary of the Rio Grande. Being late May, the river could be treacherous. If it was a week later, I wouldn't even consider taking you on it."

"When Sal took me out on it, it was winter. The water was slower. I hadn't thought about it being spring now."

"We'll be in for a much more dangerous ride than you had the last time. It'll be fairly swift."

"You don't have to go with me," she said, sitting up in her seat and facing him. "If you're doing this out of some sort of guilt about my brother, I release you of any duty you still feel."

He huffed. "You know how to get right to the point too."

"Life is too short to beat around the bush. I'm serious, Bard. You're free to go."

He leaned closer to her, their faces mere inches apart. "What if my wanting to help you has nothing to do with your brother? Perhaps the guilt I had over how I treated your brother's situation drove me to Santa Fe, but sometime between last night and this moment, I can honestly say Tru Butler is the farthest thing from my mind right now. The only thing I am thinking about is finding this man who wants to hurt you, whether he's a friend of yours or not, and making sure he's locked away for a very long time. It's the only thing driving me now." Even as Bard said this, another reason stirred within him. Catching a killer was enough to get him going, but it was this petite, creative and beautiful woman staring at him with her bright green eyes that would never let him stop.

He watched her swallow hard as her gaze averted to a place on his shirt. "If that's the case, then thank you," she said. "I just didn't want you to feel obligated."

He reached to lift her chin and bring her attention back to him. "You're not a charity case. I know we just met yesterday, but, Luci, I consider you a friend. And it has nothing to do with your brother. I'll be honest, I'm struggling with not tracking down Sal and forcing him to tell me what he knows. I'm used to getting my bad guys, so you'll have to give me a little grace. I really am trying to be more objective. In my line of work, that could slow me down and get people killed. At the same time, however, I believe you know things, but I want to give you the benefit of the doubt."

Her lips twisted into a half smile. "And I look forward to proving you wrong about Sal." She frowned. "If he's still alive. This is all so surreal." She shook her head and looked like she was about to cry.

Bard reached back for her face. "Hey, I'm sorry." He held her cheek. "I'm not being fair to you. You're not another cop who I can talk shop with. Looks like I have something else to work on. Talking honestly doesn't have to be brutal. I need to remember that."

She turned her face into his hand and closed her eyes, her long lashes brushing against her cheeks. "And yet, all I want *is* honesty. I want everything out in the open." She opened her eyes and looked directly at him. "Don't stop being honest with me. No matter how much I complain, don't stop. Promise me."

"All right." Bard heard the hesitation in his voice. Something told him this came from more than just these events. "Sometimes, people think they have your best interests at heart by keeping you in the dark. Is that what happened with your parents? Is that what caused the divide between you and them?"

She turned her face away, and he dropped his hand to his lap. "I don't want to talk about that. It's much more than keeping me in the dark. It's also forgetting that they left me there." She reached for the door handle. "We should get going."

"Wait." Bard reached for her arm to stop her. "Let me go out first and make sure the place is clear. Getting you into hiding can't come soon enough." He carefully stepped from his car and scanned the area of the parking lot. Most people had left for work already, and the lot only had a few parked cars that were familiar to him. He walked to the end of the complex and back to the other side. When he returned to the car, he stepped up to the passenger door and opened it.

Luci stepped out and, together with Hero, they walked to his apartment. Inside, he grabbed two backpacks filled with climbing gear and dehydrated food packets. Being an investigator for BLM always meant he had to be ready for a trek into the wilderness. He attached two sleeping bags to the backpacks and passed one over to her. As she inserted her arms through the straps and fit it to her back, he stocked his own with ammunition for his weapon.

"I'll make sure we do a lesson when we get out there. You're going to need to know how handle this."

She gave a quick nod of understanding as she tightened the backpack's strap around her waist. "In a perfect world, my brothers would've taught me." She didn't elaborate on the meaning behind her words, and Bard let them go.

"We need to stay focused in the present. Do you understand me?" he asked her. When she didn't reply, he stepped up to her and cupped her face in his hands. "Every decision will lead to either life or death. What's your choice?"

She took a deep breath and nodded. "Life."

Bard smiled down at her, so proud of her. She was one tough cookie. "You might be petite, but you have a ton of grit, Luci." He leaned down to plant a kiss on her forehead, only in the next second, his lips met hers.

It was short but powerful enough for him to drop his hands and step back from her in an instant, unsure of what just happened.

Luci covered her lips as her eyes widened with the same shock he felt.

"I'm s—" Bard started to apologize but stopped abruptly.

"You're what?" she said, her hand still over her mouth.

Bard picked up his backpack and secured it to his back. "Nothing." He snapped the waist strap, then looked at her. She still waited for him to explain what just happened.

Only he wasn't sure. There was only one thing he was sure of, and that was that kissing Luci, however quick it was, felt perfect. He headed toward the door, meeting Hero sitting there with his head cocked and inquisitive eyes on them both. *So many questions, huh, boy?*

Bard turned back and looked directly at Luci and said, "You said you wanted total honesty, right?" he asked.

She nodded. "Absolutely."

"Then I'm not sorry."

Luci knew she lifted her lips to Bard's when he leaned down to kiss her forehead. It all happened so fast that all she could remember was the look of admiration and pride on his face right beforehand. Pride and admiration that had been directed toward her. He'd said she had grit, but if he knew the truth, he would know she was just a girl wanting to be noticed. And if not her, then her work.

But Bard noticed *her*.

And I kissed him.

She could stand in his living room all day long questioning her part in the kiss, but deep down she knew the truth. And she knew she should apologize.

"Are you ready?" he called from the kitchen. "I've

packed enough dog food for a week. I want you to keep Hero once I get you to the cabin." Bard returned to the doorway with his dog wagging his tail beside him. Hero glanced back and forth between the two of them, eagerly awaiting that food his owner had just packed up for him.

"Bard?" Luci chewed on her lower lip in indecision. She knew she should come clean. "I want to be honest too."

"Okay…about what?"

"About what just happened."

He sighed. "Don't worry about it. Nothing will come of it. I promise. I would never do that to my friend. We need to get going." He stepped back to let her pass.

Luci hesitated for a moment, wondering if the friend he was talking about was her or Tru. But then she pushed the event off to the side to focus on the matter at hand: staying alive.

EIGHT

Bard closed up the tailgate of his pickup truck after tying down the inflatable raft and securing their supplies. He came around to the driver's seat and hopped in. Hero sat on the back seat and looked out the front window between the front seats. He gave his dog a little scratch beneath his chin and was rewarded with a wagging tail and a hanging tongue of joy. He put his paw on the passenger seat.

Both Bard and Luci had changed into wet suits at a rest area bathroom, and as she climbed into the passenger side, he noticed her sitting close to her door and away from Hero. It dawned on Bard that she might not like his dog.

Bard buckled in. "I need you to get used to him. He'll be staying with you in the cabin. I won't leave you alone."

"I know. He's just so big. To you it may not seem like it because you're big too. But to me, I think his tail could knock me over."

Bard laughed. "Possibly, but you can guarantee he'll be there to help you up. He's a good dog."

Luci eyed Hero and offered a nervous smile. Hero

glanced at him and back at her, and then he tilted his head and butted it against Luci's.

As Bard laughed again, Luci pulled away quickly. He reached up to pet his dog's head. "Gentle, boy. Some people need to be approached a little more tenderly."

Luci scoffed. "Being distrustful doesn't make me weak."

Bard started his truck's engine. "I didn't say you were weak. In fact, the strongest people still need a little tenderness. Nothing wrong with that." He backed out of the parking space and out onto the road. "Okay, where to?"

Luci rolled her pretty green eyes at him but opened the paper map of the forest and spread it out on her lap. She showed him the directions to the parking lot that they would leave the truck in before moving the rest of the way on feet and water. "I've only been here once before, so bear with me. I'll try not to get us lost."

"We have enough supplies to survive out there if we do. I also have a satellite radio to call a ranger station as well."

"Sounds like you've thought of everything." She refolded the map and put it beside them. "I know I said I could do this myself, but what do I know about surviving in the wilderness? I might've learned more from my brothers had they been around as I grew older. But that just didn't happen. After the age of fourteen, I just spent most of my time in my room painting the trees instead of trekking through them outside. Hardly the same thing."

"Hardly." He smirked her way as he drove into the forest and toward the destination she'd shown him on the map. "But give yourself some credit, Luci. I know you thought about losing me, but you were wise enough not to. I admire that."

"What would you have done if I did?" She tilted her head.

He bit back a laugh. "As if you could." In the next second, he felt her punch his bicep, and instant pain and numbness went through his arm. "Ouch!" He dropped his arm as he lost all feeling in it. "How did you know right where to hit me?"

"I just told you I have two older brothers. They may not have had a chance to teach me how to survive in the wilderness, but they did teach me how to survive on the streets."

Bard shook his arm to bring back feeling. "I'll remember that next time." He smiled her way, growing more impressed with her with every passing moment. "I can't let your size fool me, that's for sure."

"I may be small, but I'm quick and light on my feet."

"I know. Don't forget I watched you lift a painting and sprint out the front door and disappear into the shadows of Santa Fe."

"Ah-ha! So you do admit that I can lose you if I want to."

"Sure, and I'll find you just as easy as I did the last time."

Luci flashed a beautiful smile his way. "True that. Maybe your investigative skills aren't *that* bad."

It wasn't a compliment, but he would take it. They drove on in a more companionable silence and soon pulled into the parking lot where they would leave the truck behind. Bard stepped out first and whistled for Hero to follow him out the driver's door. The lot had a handful of parked cars in various spots. Some looked like their owners had left them days ago to backpack through the wilderness.

Luci stepped up beside him as he opened the door to his truck bed. He passed over her backpack, and they both secured them to their backs. He also handed her a life jacket for when they reached the water. He had one for him and Hero as well.

Closing the truck up, he put the raft under one arm and waved for her to lead the way. "After you, Squirt."

"Only Tru can call me that." She gave him a warning glare and headed toward the river trail.

"How about Tiny?" he asked to her retreating back. Her backpack practically swallowed her up. He could only see the top of her spiky hair.

She stopped quickly and turned around, but before she could respond with the annoyance her face displayed, Bard heard the snap of a twig off to his right.

He mumbled, "Keep moving and don't stop for any reason." He shifted his gaze to his right to tell her someone was there.

Her annoyed look vanished as understanding of the situation reflected back at him. She quickly turned back around and picked up her steps, proving she was extremely light on her feet. He ran along with her, but with the raft, he struggled to keep up.

"Stay low," he called in a harsh whisper, picking up his steps in case he needed to shield her from a bullet. The river loomed ahead of them, but would they have enough time to reach it? Hero stuck by his side, but Bard directed him to guard Luci. The dog raced ahead and caught up with her.

Bard needed to get his gun out, but with the raft slipping from under his arm, he dared not let it go. They would need it once they reached the water. Holding on with both hands, he ran as fast as he could, scanning the banks of the river for a place to launch.

"I'm coming up behind you. Head to the right. As soon as the raft lands in the water, jump in."

Luci kept running without turning around. "What about you?" she called out.

"I'm right behind you, but if I lose you, just get down the river. Keep Hero by your side."

He raced forward into a clearing and passed her. He scanned the tree line behind them. All seemed still, but he knew someone was in there. He reached the water and lowered the raft into the swift-moving river. He threw his life jacket in and gripped the raft with both hands as Luci came running up and jumped in with Hero.

"You have to come with us!" she shouted over the roaring water, gripping on to the side of the raft.

"Get your vest on!" Bard held on to the raft with all his strength. If he let go with one hand, he wasn't sure if he could hold on. As Luci removed her backpack and inserted her arms into the life jacket, he shouted through gritted teeth, "I'll find you down the river!"

"No!"

Before Bard knew what Luci was about to do, she leaned over the side of the raft and grabbed hold of a hanging branch. The raft slipped from one of his fingers in the sudden movement and yanked her nearly out of the raft.

In the next second, Hero bit down on the back of Luci's life jacket, keeping her in the raft.

Bard knew he had mere seconds to let go of the raft and jump in. One wrong slip and the raft would go off without him. But before he could make his move, a gunshot rang out through the air.

"Get down!" he yelled, crouching low himself. He had been right. Someone had been in the woods with them. And now they were within shooting distance.

With no time to think, Bard launched himself forward in the water, and as soon as his feet left the ground, the raft took him with it. His own backpack covered him as he struggled to slide farther into the raft in the fast-running water.

Two more shots rang through the air, but with the unpredictable direction of the rapids, their raft circled about and shifted in different directions. In the next second, he felt Luci's hands under his arms, as she pulled him farther into the raft until his body was inside fully.

Even though the three of them stayed low inside the raft, Bard knew the material wouldn't stop a bullet. Thankfully, the water put more and more distance between them and the gunman by the second, and soon, they knew they had escaped from him.

Bard sat up in the raft to scan the area as the water took them down the Rio Chama. "I don't see anyone following us down the water. That doesn't mean we're in the clear though. Do you have that map still?"

Luci remained low, but she opened her backpack, removed the folded up map and handed it over to him. "If he has a car, he can continue the drive down to the next lot. But we'll be off the water between here and there. The cabin is located at about three quarters of the way to the next lot. That second lot is actually closer to the cabin, but we can't ride upstream."

"No, but he can run up if he knows where we're going." Bard watched Luci's face for an inclination she might know if this were the case. As far as he could see, she alerted to having no knowledge of this fact.

"I don't see how he could. We haven't told anybody," she said. "Can I sit up yet?"

Bard took one last sweep around the serene forest. A multitude of conifer trees lined the embankments, and high rock cliffs stood high behind them. He scanned the top of the rocks to be sure there wasn't anyone up there, but from his view, it appeared they were all alone.

"We need to start paddling and get to the edge of the river. When it's time to get out, we have to act quickly." He watched the water ahead of them and could see rocks protruding out of the riverbed. The water moved them around the rocks and down in sweeping motions. Unhooking the paddles from inside the raft, he gave one to her as she sat up to take it.

"The water really is a lot faster this time," she shouted over the roaring rapids.

"That's because you were here during the winter. We're getting the snow melt off now. We really don't belong out here. Just one week later, this wouldn't have been possible. It still might not be." Bard kept his concerns to himself, but he had to be honest. Right now, the water was being merciful and guiding them around rocks. "Do you pray?"

She shot him a quick look and frowned. "Yeah, I do. Why?"

"Because we could use some prayers."

Luci looked back at the water coming at them. He watched her take a deep breath and blow it out slowly. "God, You're probably really tired of hearing from me, and I'm not even sure if You hear me, never mind see me. But we need Your help. Especially at the bend."

"The bend?" Bard wondered what she meant. When she wouldn't look at him, he knew they were heading right into more danger. And this time, there would be no getting away from it.

Luci knew the bend wasn't much farther. It was a treacherous turn that if they didn't maneuver just right, they could be sent over the rapids to a bed of rocks. When Sal had brought her and his wife down the river during the winter, the water had been moving much slower. He had been able to stay to the right and avoid the drop-off. Luci had yet to turn around and face Bard. Had she realized the speed of the water, she wouldn't have put them in this danger. She hated to think what would have happened to her if she tried to do this on her own. She doubted she would have made it this far, but even if she had, there's no way she would have been able to handle the raft at the bend.

"Talk to me, Luci," Bard said from the back of the raft. As she worked the left side of the raft to keep them away from the rocks on that side, he worked the right side to do the same. But he would need to know what he had to do at the bend.

She glanced over her shoulder and saw Hero lying low in the raft. She looked past the dog to his master and did her best not to show her fright.

"You'll know it when we see it. Do whatever you can to stay on the right side of the river."

"What happens if I don't?"

There was no sense dragging it out. As Luci pushed her paddle against a rock to push them away from it, she said, "We go over the falls. It's not a big drop, but there're a lot of rocks at the bottom."

"Great," he said. She looked over her shoulder and saw him swipe the spraying water from his eyes with his arm before returning to maneuvering through the river with the paddle. At the back of the raft, he took the brunt of the splashes against the rocks.

"I guess we shouldn't have come," she said. She faced forward again and moved her paddle to go right and avoid a lot of white water on the left.

"We'll get through this. It's going to be fine," he said. When she didn't respond, he called out to her, "I mean it, Luci."

Instant guilt flooded her as fast as the Rio Chama pushed them downstream. She knew that she wouldn't have survived without him today. Or yesterday, for that matter.

Suddenly, the water smoothed out, but she could see the river turning ahead and knew the bend was on the way. Luci quickly turned and faced Bard. "Whatever happens, I just want you to know that I am grateful that you showed up in my life last night. I may not have treated you kindly, but it's just because I don't trust anyone. So thank you for not turning me in or leaving me behind."

Bard looked behind her shoulder, then back at her. "It's that bad?"

"It was bad in the winter." She let her excuse hang there as the raft took them closer to the approaching bend.

Suddenly, the current picked up and turned them sideways. Luci faced forward again and fought the river with her paddle. She cut into the green-brown depths with fast strokes, leaning a bit over the edge for more leverage.

"Get ready!" she yelled as water sprayed into her

mouth and into her eyes. When the raft picked up and tilted to the right, she let out a scream. As they landed, a swell sprayed up over them like a deluge, filling the raft. Hero managed to push himself lower to the bottom of the raft, tucking his large body into the corner for protection. "Switch sides and push with me to stay away from the other side."

She trusted that Bard was doing just that as the raft wanted to go straight, and they had to work together to turn to the right and avoid the drop-off. She used every ounce of strength she had in her to continue to chop into the water over and over and over again to keep the raft pointed and moving in the other direction.

A few times, she thought she heard herself crying but they were sounds more out of straining her body and pushing it to the limits. She could see why rafting wasn't allowed in the spring and summer here.

"You're doing great!" Bard hollered. "Don't stop!" His voice sounded muffled as water doused their faces.

Then finally, the other side of the river became trees again and they skirted the danger zone. The river now swept them away from it toward a safer and much tamer area.

Luci fell back into the raft and gripped Hero's fur. It was the first time she touched him, but if he minded, he didn't let on. She leaned into him while her rapid breathing subsided and her heart rate returned to normal. Then she turned and faced Bard and found him wearing the biggest smile directed at her.

"That was fun. Wanna do it again?" His hazel eyes twinkled with the light.

Luci dropped her paddle in the raft and launched

herself at him, wrapping her arms around his neck, ecstatic that they had just made it through unscathed.

With her life jacket on, she couldn't feel his arms around her but knew they were there. She had her cheek against the pulse of his neck and could feel that he had experienced the same adrenaline rush she had.

Shaking her head against his, she said, "Thank you. Thank you. Thank you. I could not have done that without you. And no. I don't want to do that again."

"Good. Neither do I." His voice rumbled low against her ear. "But it's done, and I'm so proud of you. You are stronger than you think you are."

Luci felt his hand behind her head, and she pulled back to look into his face. He really was a handsome man. But his validation of her made him so attractive.

As they hit clear water, the sounds of the rushing rapids disappeared, and all she could hear was their breathing. She knew she should move out of his arms but instead found herself resting her cheek in his shoulder.

With her face turned away from his, she said, "I haven't felt strong since I was fourteen years old. After my brother's accident, my parents' marriage imploded, and they fought all the time. There was nothing I could do to stop it. I was completely powerless. If I'm strong now, it's only because I had to figure out how to survive on my own. I was invisible the moment my brother woke up and didn't remember any of us."

"Invisible. That just boggles my mind because you light up a room. You're stunning."

Luci lifted her head to face Bard. Their eyes locked with an intensity that made her feel seen. She lifted her hand to his cheek, brushing against his day-old stubble.

"I mean it, Luci. You are beautiful inside and out."

His gaze dropped to her lips, and she felt her heart rate escalate again in anticipation. This time she would let him make the move to kiss her. But just as Bard leaned down, a gunshot blasted through the air, and he threw her to the bottom of the raft to cover her.

In the next second, air rushed from the raft and water flooded in. As the raft sunk, the shooter had full range of them.

NINE

Bard grabbed his gun from the side compartment of his backpack. He had it wrapped up in a plastic bag but quickly removed it. "Take this," he said, thrusting the handle end at Luci. She stared at it as if it would burn her. "Now. I have to get us to the edge and out of the water, and I need you to cover me." She lifted a shaky hand from the growing water in the raft and took it. He thought she might drop it, so he took her hand and positioned it with a secure grip over the weapon. Looking her in the eyes, he said, "You can do this. I have faith in you. And in God who you prayed to. He'll lead us to safety, while you guard my back. I know you can do this, Luci."

Her teeth chattered, probably more from fear than the frigid water that had been snow only days ago, but she nodded multiple times. They both knew while they struggled to stay afloat, a killer was setting up his next shot. The only good thing was the river was moving them away at a faster clip than he could run through the trees.

Even being out of the rapids, the water was swift and strong. The added threat of being shot at had him struggling on where to put his focus. If he got shot, Luci would be out here on her own. He hoped the fear of that idea didn't show on his face. He couldn't let her lose her confidence already. After she had just confided in him, all he wanted to do was rescue her. He wanted her to be safe, but more than anything, he wanted Luci to go on and live a life where she wasn't invisible anymore.

Even if at the moment, he wished she was. He wished they were all invisible to the shooter at this point. But instead, they were out here in the middle of the river with nothing to shield them from flying bullets coming their way. Their deflating raft became more useless by the second. If the bullets didn't get them, death by drowning definitely could.

Bard couldn't let either happen. Luci needed to go on and make a name for herself with her art. If she died today, he would never forgive himself. With his own determination set, he scanned the river ahead for something that would give them leverage. Cutting through the water with his paddle, he made his way closer to the edge with quick strokes. In his concentration to reach a tree limb protruding out over the water, he knew he made himself more exposed to the gunman. He looked back at Luci, only to find her sitting up and aiming a gun at the tree line.

"Get down!" he whispered harshly.

"How can I have your back if I'm flat on my face? Just get us out of this raft and let *me* do my part."

Bard didn't like it, but she was right. Knowing she was exposed only made him more determined to reach that limb. He would have one chance to grab it, while at the same time holding on to the raft to keep it from slipping any farther downstream—and taking Luci and Hero with it, not to mention all their supplies.

Bard took a quick calculation of the speed of the river and estimated he had about three seconds between a boulder coming up and the branch. As he passed by the large rock on the water's edge, he braced himself for the three seconds and, on the second one, leaped into the air with one arm up and one arm holding on to the edge of the raft.

His fingers cut into the sharp bark of the tree branch, but he made secure contact with a tight grip. He whistled, and Hero jumped up onto the limb. Bard managed to swing a leg up and lie down on the branch while still holding on to the raft. A glance down showed Luci was too short and couldn't reach no matter how hard she tried.

Bard knew that he could extend his hand down to help her, but that would mean letting the raft go. It was one or the other—the choice was an easy one to make.

In a split second, he let the raft go and grabbed hold of her arm, lifting her up and onto the branch.

"Bard, our supplies!" Lucy's face expressed the gravity of the situation. Their food, beds, phones and map had been in their packs. The only thing they had left was his gun that Luci still held in her hand.

"I had to make a choice, and I don't regret the one I made."

On a sigh, she rested her forehead on the tree limb, exhaustion and disappointment showing through her every movement. "What are we going to do now?"

Bard reached over and took the gun from her hand. With the trees, he knew they were shielded from view, but it wouldn't be long before the shooter caught up to them. "We start running."

She lifted her face and locked her gaze on his. "To where? I don't know where we are. I don't know if we passed the place to get out or if the cabin is still farther down the river."

"Hopefully it's down the river because we're not walking back toward the shooter."

"It's already getting dark," she stated the obvious that he had been avoiding. "If the shooter doesn't get us, there are plenty other elements that will."

All Bard could do was nod. She was right, and it was his fault.

All the trees looked the same. Every direction Luci turned gave her no clue of the whereabouts of the cabin. All she remembered was that Sal's artist retreat had been soon after the bend. But in their struggle of being shot at and then focusing on surviving, meant they could have already passed the point where they were supposed to disembark.

Bard stood with his oversized dog, studying the dark trees to their left. He held his gun at the ready in front of him. "Luci, you have to make a decision. This guy could already be here and watching us. I say we continue going downriver. We can't risk going back up and running into him. What do you want to do?"

There was something different about Bard. The moment they stepped off that branch and climbed down the tree to the forest floor, he'd yet to give a firm direction and seemed even a bit hesitant to.

"Why are you leaving the decision up to me?" she asked.

He frowned but wouldn't look at her. He just kept his

eyes to the trees. "I've never second-guessed my decisions before, but lately, I've been really messing up. I'm beginning to think you're right, and I'm not really good at this job."

Luci thought back to the moment in her studio when she had accused him of being a poor investigator. "I didn't mean what I said. I'm sorry I said it in the heat of the moment. You're a fine investigator. Now make a decision."

He moved his gaze from the trees and captured hers. "Even if I put you in more danger? I came here to protect you, but instead I've allowed the situation to escalate and put you at more risk."

"I would have come on my own anyway. And most likely I'd be dead by now if you hadn't been here. The bullets may not have hit me, but I would never have made it to that branch. You saw me struggling to reach it. You had a decision to make, me or the supplies. I'm grateful you chose me. Now make another one. This is no time to wallow in self-pity."

He swallowed convulsively, but after quickly looking behind her again, he straightened and said, "We go downriver. You go first with Hero. I'll be right behind you. If we've already passed Sal's cabin, we'll figure that out tomorrow. Right now, I need to find a suitable shelter for the night. I'm sorry to say you're not going to like it."

Luci sidled up next to Hero and headed in the direction Bard pointed. "Don't forget, I'm homeless now. Anything is appreciated." When she looked back and saw him pick up a long stick, she knew she would be roughing it tonight. Luci wondered if she would even be alive in the morning. After every bout with danger in the last day, she was beginning to not take every breath for granted. With only the wet suits, she felt the chill of the night set in. She kept her thoughts to herself, not wanting to give Bard another thing to worry about. They may have been in the desert, but with no sun to heat them, the temperature grew colder with each passing minute.

Luci walked on, every so often getting a direction from Bard. She could barely hear him walking and had to look a few times to see if he was still there.

"For someone of your size, you walk with a light foot," she said.

"For someone of your size, you don't. I figure you're making enough noise for the both of us."

Luci stopped quickly and turned. "I do not," she said and then froze. She saw no sign of him now. "Bard?" she whispered.

"I'm over here. To your left." He spoke so low that she barely heard him.

Luci moved to her left and finally found his silhouette by a tree. She saw he had multiple branches now. "Why did you stop?"

"I noticed a clearing. We'll camp here." He began to lean the branches against a large tree, and after breaking off a few more from the tree, he created a leaning shelter.

"I don't think you're going to fit in that."

"And you would be right. It's just for you." He whistled for his dog, who approached him and sat obediently. "Guard," Bard gave the command and then said to her, "Climb inside." When she did, he continued, "I'll be circling the perimeter through the night. Do your best to get comfortable and get some shut-eye."

She peered through the large sticks and watched him turn to leave the clearing. "Wait. What about you? You've been up already for more than forty-eight hours. We should take turns."

"Get some rest." It was his only response before he left the clearing, giving her no room for discussion. Within seconds, she couldn't make him out in the dark any longer.

"Bard, I'm sorry," she called out fast. She couldn't help but think his sudden distance was because of what she had said about his investigative skills. "It was wrong of me to say something so rude to you. I know now you are a good investigator. Please forgive me."

After a few moments of silence, she began to think he had already left the vicinity. Then he spoke low.

"What if my quick judgment of people has nothing to do with my experience on the streets with criminals and more to do with my distrust of people?"

Luci heard a raw pain in his voice that she never would have thought would come from such a strong man. She weighed her words, not wanting to speak and cause more pain to him. She didn't know what to say, but she did know that he was trusting her with a deep secret. She was certain not even Tru knew this about Bard. She didn't feel honored, but rather concerned. For Bard to reveal such a private part of himself, he had to be worried about something.

"Why do you distrust people?" She spoke quietly and wasn't sure if he was even close enough to hear her.

When he spoke again, he had moved to the other side of the clearing. He obviously was circling the their camp as he said he would. "I guess I learned early on people were never what they said they were, unless it was convenient for them. My dad was a politician. I was only his son for photo ops. I suppose it tainted me and instilled this idea that people acted out of motive only. I'm doing the best I can, Luci, to not be so cynical. I know there are genuinely good people in the world. I consider you one of them."

Luci smiled into the darkness. "I consider you one too."

He didn't respond again, and as the night grew darker and quieter, she knew the conversation was over.

Luci also knew she was supposed to be sleeping but being curled up on the hard ground behind her sticks didn't allow her to relax enough to even close her eyes.

After repeatedly moving around to get comfortable, she heard a huff and turned to see Hero at the opening.

She put her hand up. "You can't fit in here either. Don't even think about it."

In the next second, the dog circled around three times before dropping down by the opening. He lifted his head and his eyes glistened in the dim moonlight. Then he lowered it down to sleep. He lifted his head again and looked at her. Suddenly, Luci realized he was giving her a message.

Lay her head on him.

She didn't know how she felt about that. It wasn't a thought she jumped on, but after a few yawns, she turned and slowly laid down with her head on his side. She felt guilty that Bard was out guarding while she could sleep. She kept herself awake out of that guilt until she felt herself losing the battle with exhaustion.

"Bard?" she whispered, but no response came back. She wondered why he wasn't answering her and figured she had upset him. As her eyes fell closed and she had no energy to open them again, the idea that he could be in trouble crossed her mind. But surely, she would've heard something if he was.

Wouldn't she?

TEN

Bard knew the gunman wasn't far. He also knew that if he stayed too close to Luci, he would lead the guy right to her. He had chosen the clearing because it wasn't directly on the path they had been on, but rather through a thick brush of trees. He didn't want to go too far from her either but had to trust that Hero would alert him if a stranger was in their midst. The fact was he trusted his dog more than he did people.

Bard couldn't believe that he had shared his deepest weakness with Luci. This little sprite of a girl—*no*, not girl. Woman. He couldn't let her size fool him. She was a full-grown woman even if she was a fraction of his size. And she definitely undid something in him. In the deep, dark night, while he hid her away, he wondered how she had managed to slip into the cracks of his own shelter and expose his hang-up. At thirty years old, he should have been well past the effects of an absent and opportunistic father. Luci had asked him why he was so cynical. But it wasn't until he'd slipped up with her brother that he realized it was a problem. He had always believed he had good intuition. He always got his bad guy.

And he would get this one too, he vowed. Friend of Luci's or not.

Bard held his gun at the ready and stepped soundlessly across the forest floor. He wondered when the guy planned to make his move. There was no way he'd followed them this far, only to leave them. Bard wondered if the guy had been able to cross the river. Perhaps that's what prolonged him from reaching them. He had to cross over down the river and work his way back up to them. There was a good chance he wouldn't even find them. Bard could only hope.

His body screamed for sleep, but Bard rejected its plea. There was no way he would let his guard down. He may have been cynical, but he wasn't stupid. This guy was expecting him to have to rest at some point. Bard needed to keep his adrenaline up. Listening to every forest sound helped with that. Any of the sounds he heard could have been the shooter, or it could have been any number of the other kind of predators. He would let Luci sleep for a little while, but with a forest full of animals soon on the prowl for their food in predawn, it couldn't be for long.

He heard a sharp intake of breath off to his right. Bard froze as he turned an ear in the direction, wondering if Luci had come out of hiding. In the next second, a crunching sound pulled his attention to the left. Bard brought his gun up and held it with both hands. A moment later, a short laugh came from behind.

Bard whipped around and pointed his gun into the darkness. Either his shooter knew how to throw his voice, or Bard was being surrounded. With all his ammunition downriver, that only left him with the bullets that had already been in his Glock. His magazine held fifteen rounds. Another sound behind him told him there were at least four men coming in his direction, and they probably had a lot more ammo between the four of them.

He hoped it wasn't more than four.

Bard slowly dropped to the ground. He didn't need to make himself a standing target. Slowly, he shimmied toward some brush and down a drop-off. The leaves were wet and soggy, so hiding in them wasn't an option, but he stayed close to the trunk of a tree and sat up to lean against it. He brought his gun back and positioned it out in front.

"Where'd he go?" A harsh whisper came from above where Bard had been standing moments before.

"It's too dark." A light flashed on and illuminated the area above. "I don't care about him. It's the girl we need. Find her. I'll take care of him."

One set of footsteps passed by the tree on the other side of him. Bard turned his face to see the back of the man for a brief moment before he slipped into the trees. Thankfully, he wasn't going in the direction of Luci. But how long would it be before he did? For now, though, Bard focused on the fact that there had only been two voices. Unless a third or fourth man wasn't speaking, it had just been the two of them coming near. They probably each threw sounds to confuse him. And now with one gone, Bard would just be up against the one that remained.

"All we want is the painting," the man's voice carried down from above. "Tell us where it is, and we'll let you both go."

Bard didn't believe that for a second. But he wanted to know why they needed this painting so much. Could a few bricks of cocaine really be worth all of this? Despite his curiosity, he kept his lips sealed. These men were just a couple of operatives, working for someone in power.

Suddenly, Bard realized why they hadn't been shot when they were in the raft. The raft had been shot, but not them. These men needed them alive to get what they wanted.

A painting by a no-name artist?

It didn't make sense. If it was the drugs they were looking for, those were also now downriver, probably caught up on a rock in the twisted, deflated raft somewhere.

The ground above him crunched.

Bard slowly turned his face and looked up through his eyelashes to see the dark shadow behind the blaring flashlight of a cell phone.

"There you are," the man said with a sick chuckle. He raised his arm, and Bard didn't have to see the man to know he held a gun on him.

But why would the guy kill him now after letting him live all day?

Knowing this allowed Bard to slowly get up with his hands raised. "I'll do whatever you want," Bard said, having no inclination to follow through on that offer. But he thought it was the best way to engage the man in some conversation that would answer some questions he had.

"Who are you?" the man asked.

"I'm just a friend." He thought it best to not alert the man to his occupation. "The woman is my friend's sister. I'd love to know why you're after her."

"You don't ask the questions. I do. Now drop the gun, and you can tell me where she is." When Bard hesitated, the man said, "Now. I won't ask again. And all we need is her. Not you."

Then Bard had been right. He probably hadn't been shot in the raft because they needed to make sure she survived the river ride. He probably would not survive this conversation once the man had what he needed, not that he was going to give the gunman any information.

Bard let the gun go, and it landed in the leaves with a thud. "There. Now you're the only one with a weapon."

"Kick it away."

Bard did as he was told, watching it disappear into the darkness.

"Good. Now where is she?"

"She lost me. She used me to get across the river, and as soon as we made it, she ran off. She even took my dog. Can you believe that? She's protecting somebody." Bard had to think that his words weren't too far from the truth. He knew Luci had thought about ditching him, and he knew she was covering for someone too.

"Then I guess I don't have any use for you."

Bard had less than a second to make his move. In the thigh compartment of his tactical pants, he would have had a knife, but in a wet suit, all he had were his hands.

But the man had a gun, and Bard meant to get it from him. Crouching low, Bard heard the gunshot go off above him as he rammed at the midsection of the man. Plowing forward with all his strength, he knocked the guy back and to the ground, making a grab for the weapon and twisting the guy's arm backward.

It blasted again, shaking Bard to the core. They both paused for a split second. Bard took a quick mental check of his body but felt no pain.

Then the man went limp in Bard's hold, and the gun

stayed in his hand as he released the guy. Bard rolled over, seeking the cell phone with its light still blaring in the leaves. The guy must have dropped it when Bard rammed into him.

Bard brought the light over to the guy and saw he was dead, shot at the back of his head by his own gun. He checked the man's pockets for ammo and found a magazine filled. Taking that, the weapon and his own Glock found in the leaves below, Bard left him with his cell phone on his chest. With no service out in the forest, taking it was pointless. Bard could only hope when they got to Sal's cabin, he would find some sort of radio system set up that they could use to call for help. Plus, Bard didn't want to be tracked by whoever was already using the cell phone to track this guy.

Now to find his buddy. Bard set out into the dark wilderness in the direction the man had gone. He had to find him before the guy found Luci.

But an hour later, Bard found no sign of the creep, and as he stepped back into the clearing with the shelter, he also found no sign of Luci or Hero.

The soles of Luci's water shoes slapped against the forest floor, keeping cadence with the rapid beat of her heart. She ran alone as Hero had gone after the intruder who had found the encampment. She could still hear the echoing sounds of the gunshots that had rung out through the forest and had awoken her just in time. The first shot had caused both her and the dog to jump to their feet and run out of the makeshift lean-to. It took Luci a few moments to realize Hero had gone after someone. Luci ran in the opposite direction, but now she raced blindly in the dense wilderness.

As the sky lightened to a gray, she knew night was over, but that didn't mean the danger had ended. And where was Bard?

The second gunshot she had heard brought the weight of the realization that he could be dead.

A piercing pain in her side made her slow her steps and clutch her waist until it subsided. Luci slipped between a couple trees and leaned against one, doing her best to stay out of view, except she didn't know what direction someone would be coming at her. No place was safe to stand.

She looked to the sky to see if she could figure out what direction she was heading in. With no sun yet up, it was hard to tell east from west. For all she knew, she could be running in circles.

She crossed her arms in front of her to ward off the chill and realized her body craved water. She turned an ear to the sounds of the river and found she couldn't hear it anymore. Which meant she was walking away from the water, not alongside it.

"God, I need more direction. You got us through the roaring river and around that treacherous bend, but I need Your guidance again. I know even though I stand beneath the lush green leaves of the trees, You can see me. I know that I am not invisible to You. And I know You can see Bard. I ask You to lead us in the direction of each other again. And I ask You to protect him and keep him safe. I pray that it wasn't him who was shot."

The fact that bullets were flying made this whole situation escalate to a place beyond her imagination. She took a deep breath, and as she let it out, she could feel her chest trembling.

Stay focused.

At any turn, someone could jump out at her. She looked up to the trees and thought about climbing them. And then what? Wait to die?

Luci made up her mind to step back out onto the path and walk on until she found shelter. It may have been the wrong choice, and it may lead her straight into danger, but hiding in the shadows of the trees while she froze would only end her chances of survival more.

Peering up through the branches above her, she thought she saw the sky brighter on one side and hoped that meant that was east. She turned and faced south— or what she thought was south—and took her first steps. With nothing to mark her path, she knew she could very well be back at this specific spot again without realizing it.

Searching the ground below her, she found a rock that filled her palm. It had a pointy edge to it, and she scraped away some bark on a tree to her right. She walked a little farther down and did it again. If she happened to circle back to this area, she would know it.

She did her best to keep her feet light on the forest floor, not wanting to attract any attention from the men following her or from wild animals hunting for breakfast. More than anything, she wanted to call out for Bard. She wanted to scream from the top of her lungs for someone to come help her. The fact that she couldn't only made her feel more isolated in this huge wilderness. Miles and miles surrounded her in all directions as she pressed on. Then she heard a footstep that wasn't her own.

Slowly, Luci turned and came within twenty feet of a strange man. He couldn't have been more than twenty years old, but his face was worn, looking almost like leather. He had black hair that looked greasy, and his clothes were torn. Shredded, actually. Something told her an animal had done it.

She wanted to know where Hero was, but the heated anger coming from the man's eyes and his curled lip caused her throat to go dry. As they stared at each other for the briefest of seconds, she knew the race was on. At the same time, they hit the ground running. As she turned and stepped out in one move, he was quickly on her heels.

Luci knew he was mere feet behind her, but she dared not look back or slow down. She knew as soon as he got his hands on her, she was dead. The fact that he didn't just shoot her told her he had lost his gun somewhere along the way. She probably had Hero to thank for that.

Never had she run so fast without ceasing, only focusing on the sounds of his footsteps so close behind. A few times, she felt the wind of his hand reach out to her and miss her. She heard his grunts as he strained to grab hold of her. She heard her own whining in her breaths as she struggled to keep her distance from him.

And then suddenly she didn't hear him anymore.

Luci continued to run, not daring to look back, believing it to be a trick. She wondered if he moved to a different place and planned to cut her off at some point. She looked to her right and left. That's when she saw the stream of smoke. Smoke from a fire, *no*, a chimney!

Luci took the turn and headed in the direction of another living being. *It must be why the man stopped running*, she thought. He didn't want to be led to where there were people. She pressed on until finally she ran right out of the woods and faced Sal's cabin. But if there was smoke coming out of the chimney, that meant it wasn't vacant. She wondered who could be using it and if she would be welcomed.

Before she could take one step closer, the unmistakable click of a gun to her right gave her her answer. With her heart already beating in her chest from her run, Luci turned and caught her breath at the sight of Sal pointing a gun at her.

ELEVEN

Bard touched the bark of another tree that had been carved on. Someone had been through this way, judging by the fresh gouge. It had to be Luci, he figured. He hadn't seen anyone else out here in his quest to find her and his dog. He would have whistled, but he didn't want Hero to leave Luci's side.

Crouching down, he touched the earth and could tell leaves and dirt had been disturbed. He found a small footprint tread and could tell the direction she'd been heading in. He stood and went that way. He could also tell a second person had been with her.

Or rather, *after* her.

As Bard made his way in the direction of the footprints, he half expected to find her body along the path. Something he also noticed was that his dog's footprints were *not* with hers. His hope that Hero had been protecting her diminished with each step. He braced himself for the worst. The only good thing was knowing they wanted something from her, and so they might keep her alive.

He still couldn't believe they would go to these lengths for one of her paintings, or even the bricks of cocaine. The fact they were demanding the painting and not the drugs told him there was something about the painting that made them nervous.

Luci had been concerned about the woman's eyes. She had painted them wrong the first time and was willing to break the law to remedy her mistake. Was it about the lady in the red dress? Was someone upset that Luci painted her?

Enough to kill Luci?

Bard pressed on, picking up his pace. He didn't want to go so fast that he lost her trail, but he also knew time was critical.

Suddenly, only her tracks remained, and the other person veered off to the left.

Bard paused at the separation and had to make a split-second decision of which direction he would continue in. Follow her tracks or go after the man in size elevens.

He took solace in seeing that her tracks continued. They could have ended right here with only the man's shoeprints a little deeper in the dirt to show he carried her out.

A glance around at the trees and leaves didn't indicate any kind of struggle occurred here. Only that she continued on at a fast pace.

Bard decided it was best to find her first. He couldn't keep her safe if they were separated. He wondered, though, what had caused the man to depart from his attack?

Bard could only think the thug would do such a thing if he knew Luci was heading straight for the man in charge of him.

These criminals ran in packs. There was no such thing as a lone wolf. If someone went rogue, they were

typically eliminated quickly. Which meant this guy's
job was to push her in a certain direction, even while
she thought she was getting away. She would have no
idea that the rest of his pack was lying in wait for her
to arrive…right into their clutches.

Bard's senses went on high alert as he moved swiftly
through the forest. His attention flitted from the left
to the right, behind him and in front of him. He didn't
think he blinked until finally he came upon one of the
pack holding a gun—right on Luci.

Bard flinched for just a second as he quickly registered the sight before him. It took him two attempts
before finally shouting, "Put the gun down!" He held
his own, aimed and ready.

The man turned quickly, also taking aim, but just
as Bard was about to pull the trigger, a loud bark came
from the left. Hero raced at full force, leaping into the
air at least ten feet from the perpetrator and landing
right on hist side like a bullet himself.

The gun flew from the man's hands as he hit the
ground with the full force of the K-9's flying body. He
screamed at the sudden impact but couldn't move one
inch with Hero's full weight on top of him.

Bard rushed forward, kicking the revolver toward
Luci. "Pick it up and point it at him," he shouted the
direction for her to take with it. "Hold," he told his dog.
Coming closer, Bard recognized the guy as the man in
the photo with Luci. The one at Sal's house.

Bard couldn't believe what he was seeing—*who* he
was seeing.

"Salazar Ramon?" Bard asked, and at the man's nod,
Bard looked to Luci. She hadn't touched the gun. It still
sat at her feet where he had kicked it. "Pick it up, Luci."

She shook her head. "I can't. I won't aim it at him."

"Even after he aimed it at you? I think you're taking your loyalty too far. And I have to wonder why." He stared intently for an explanation.

Instead, she lifted her chin with a determination that brought her to his level, if not in height, then in authority. "I will not point that thing at Sal. And you can't make me."

"This makes you look guilty, Luci." Bard had to make her see what she was doing to herself because of this high esteem she put in this lowlife.

She shrugged. "What else is new?"

Bard's heart clenched in his chest. "He could have killed you. Even accidentally."

She shook her head. "He wouldn't have. I know it." She gazed down at Sal, locked in Hero's hold. "I know you wouldn't have done it." She put her hand over her heart. "I know it in here." She looked back at Bard. "Now get your dog off him and let him up."

Bard thought his head would explode. This man was bad news, and she refused to see the truth. Everything in him told him Sal was guilty. Guilty of smuggling drugs. Guilty of setting her up to take the fall. And nearly guilty of killing her. Now she wanted him to let this creep go?

Bard looked down at Sal, bile rising in his throat at what he was about to say. "You may have her duped, but not me. I'll let you up, but I'm watching your every move. And you're not getting your gun back." Bard picked up the revolver in his free hand. To Hero, he said, "Release."

Hero let out a grunt but released his hold and jumped from the man. He stood by close, lowering his haunches to wait for his next command. Then he let out a deep bark that sounded like a warning. One wrong move, and Sal would be back on the ground.

Luci stepped forward around Bard and offered her hand to Sal.

But instead of accepting her help, the man crumpled into heart-wrenching tears. He covered his face with his arm as he cried out, "I'm so sorry. I never wanted you to get hurt."

Luci looked up at Bard with a smug expression. "See?"

"The only thing I see is a man who knows how to manipulate someone willing to die for him."

She put her arm around Sal and helped him sit up as she looked at Bard and said, "Well, you're right about one thing."

Bard could see keeping Luci alive would be a lot harder than he'd thought. Especially when she insisted on running with the wolves.

"Sal, tell me what's going on." Luci knelt by her friend. She knew she had pushed Bard too far. But she also knew she had to give Sal an opportunity to explain. A glance up at Bard hovering tall above her showed his patience had worn thin. He still held his gun on Sal, and she worried about the angry look to his eyes. Pulling her friend up, she said, "Why did you point a gun at me?"

Sal swiped at his eyes as he stood before her. He glanced to the trees around them. "It's not safe out here. Come inside."

"No," Bard answered quickly. "For all I know, we'll walk in on an ambush. We're not stepping foot in there until I have searched the place to make sure it's safe."

Sal hunched in front of her, seeming to cower away from Bard. Sal was closer to her height than to the giant lawman. Luci hated how Bard could intimidate people just by standing beside them.

"It's nothing but an artist retreat," she said. "Lots of paint and canvases."

Bard replied, "Then the search should go quickly." He stepped up to come between Luci and Sal.

Sal looked to the small cabin. It was one floor with a small loft above. Some of his painting supplies were scattered on the little porch. Because a canopy of trees covered the house, moss grew on the roof and kept it in the shadows. The place seemed unlivable, but for what he used it for, it suited him well.

"You're being ridiculous," Luci said to Bard's back.

Sal said, "Sir, I can't stress this enough. We are not safe out here. I promise you that no harm will come to you inside. I can't make that promise out here."

"He's right," Luci said. "Someone had been chasing me. He would have killed me if he caught me. I saw it in his eyes. You can trust Sal."

Luci could see Bard tense up in front of her. His shoulders rose with a couple deep breaths as he made his decision.

"Hero, guard. Luci, get to the porch and wait for me. Stay low. I'm going to check the windows with Sal. You won't be out of my eyesight." Bard waved his gun for her to start walking. As she moved forward, she noticed that the dog forced her forward from behind. Bard meant for Hero to guard *her*, or detain her?

When Bard didn't change his command, she knew it wasn't a mistake. In her support of Sal, Bard believed she was untrustworthy now too.

Luci walked to the porch as he had said and watched how Bard peeked into the windows at the front and side of the house. He came back pushing Sal toward the porch with the gun at the man's back.

"Do you really have to treat him like this?" she asked.

"I thought I was being nice." The anger in his voice threaded through his words. "If I had my way, I would have already bound him. You may be fine with being held at point-blank, but I have something to say about that."

For a brief moment, Luci thought she heard pain in his voice. But that was ridiculous.

"He didn't shoot me," she said. To Sal, she asked, "You weren't going to, either, correct? Tell him."

"I don't want to hear his response," Bard said. He waved his gun up the stairs to the door. "After you."

"Of course I wasn't going to shoot you, Luci." Sal headed up the stairs. "I just don't know who I can trust anymore." He stepped to the door, and just as he opened it, a gunshot blasted from inside, splintering the wood of the door and sending Sal to the floor.

Bard quickly turned, wrapping an arm around Luci and pulling her down.

"Drop your weapon!" he shouted into the small cabin.

The sound of a woman crying brought Luci to her knees. "Don't hurt her!" Luci shouted, reaching up for Bard's arm.

He glanced down at her quickly. "Another friend of yours who's innocent? Just how many people are you protecting? I find it interesting that the threat that had been outside is now inside. Interesting or perhaps co-ordinated would be a better word. Are you all working together?"

"Natalie! Put your weapon down," Luci said. "We're not going to hurt you. Bard, not every case is orchestrated."

As soon as she heard the gun drop to the floor with a thud, she scurried over to Sal's wife. Nat leaned up against a wall on the far side. Luci noticed blood on her leg, and Natalie was so pale and weak. Her head lolled to the side and her brown hair was a mess. As Luci approached her, she looked back at Bard to find him studying Natalie as well.

Luci wrapped her arm around the frightened and obviously injured woman. "It's going to be okay."

Natalie shook her head. "I've never been so scared in my life. They won't stop until I'm dead."

"Who?" Bard asked.

"I don't know. I really don't." Natalie dropped her head and cried quietly.

With a lift to her chin, Luci said to Bard, "Can't you see that there is always more to a story?"

Bard pressed his lips tight and breathed deep with a nod. He leaned down and pulled Sal up, while at the same time kicking the door closed behind him. "You win, Luci. All I see is I can't trust my gut anymore. And that scares me."

TWELVE

Staying low and below the two windows, Luci crawled across the floor to bring Natalie a water bottle from one of the cabinets along the wall. There were only a few in there, left from the Ramons' previous visit. Possibly the same visit that Luci had joined them on.

As Natalie took a long drink, Luci scanned the cabin. It was just as she remembered it. Sal's painting supplies took up most of the space of the one-room cabin with a loft above. Natalie had been kind enough to let Luci stay in the loft while she and Sal took the pullout sofa on the far wall below the side window. It had been tight quarters with just them, but now with big, burly Bard and his large dog, the cabin felt stifling.

Of course, the tenseness in the cabin could be from Bard's poorly controlled anger. He looked like he wanted to hit something, but judging by the last words he spoke, Luci thought that that person might be himself. He sat on the floor across the room below the window by the door, his gun in his lap. His eyes were closed, but she could tell he had an ear turned to any sounds outside. Hero slept on the floor in front of the sofa, catching up on his much-needed rest after being awake all night. The only thing Sal had said after they entered the cabin was that he didn't understand why Luci was there. He just kept saying that she wasn't supposed to be there. He sat at the table with his hands covering his face, and she didn't think she'd ever seen him look so defeated. She still believed in him, but she had to admit something didn't feel right.

Swallowing half the bottle, Natalie dropped her head to the back wall. "We don't have much food. We weren't able to prepare." Tears welled up in her eyes.

"Shh," Luci said, grabbing her hand. "We'll make do."

Natalie passed the bottle to her. "Take some. You need it too. We have a few more bottles in the cabinet."

Luci hated drinking the injured woman's water, but Natalie was right. Luci had gone without water for nearly twenty-four hours. She took the bottle and paced herself with a few sips.

Handing it back, she asked quietly, "What happened?"

Natalie looked down at her leg. "I was shot. I was at home in the kitchen getting dinner ready. Suddenly, this man barged in the back door and just shot me. Right in the leg. Sal wasn't home yet, and after the man realized that, he ran out."

Luci could tell Natalie was in borderline shock. Her face was pale, and her hands trembled, sloshing the water in the bottle. She didn't want to make the woman have to continue to explain what happened, but they needed to know.

Luci looked up at Sal. "Where were you?"

Sal dropped his hands to the table. "You have to believe me. I didn't know it was you outside. I would never have pulled my gun on you if I had known."

Luci tried to smile at her friend but failed. "I know

you wouldn't have. But I need to know what you know and where you were when Natalie was shot?"

"I'd like to know that too." Bard spoke with his eyes still closed. "If you're so innocent, then spill."

Luci watched Sal pinch his eyes to stop more tears from coming. She said, "Bard, let me ask the questions."

Sal implored her and reached a hand on the table in her direction. "I was at Jemez's apartment. I went there to discuss some work he was doing at the gallery." His lips began to tremble. "But I was too late."

"So you know Cody's dead?"

Sal nodded. "When I saw…him, I had to get home fast."

Luci tilted her head. "You didn't think to call the police?"

Sal shook his head. "I knew Jemez's death wasn't random. The man had connections, and I thought he must have made a bad deal. But then…" Sal swallowed convulsively, looking at his wife. "When I returned home to find Nat on the floor in the kitchen, all I could think was to get her out of there before they came back. I panicked. Just like I did outside with you."

Bard huffed. "Don't you mean you had to get yourself out of there? Using your wife sounds convenient to me."

"Bard," Luci cut him off from going further.

"Can't you see she's injured?" Sal yelled over her shoulder at Bard.

Bard opened his eyes and glared at Sal. "Most people would get her to a hospital. Not hide her away in a remote cabin."

"You don't understand. These people are vicious." Sal sounded desperate. "You didn't see what they did to Cody Jemez." The man's voice broke.

Bard looked across the floor at Luci. "I can imagine."

She knew he was speaking of his own fear of her meeting the same demise. She dropped her gaze to her lap, needing to stay focused. "Was Cody selling drugs through the gallery? Is that the work you went to his place to talk about?"

At Sal's quietness, Luci had her answer. He knew drugs were being moved through his gallery. But did he know how?

"How? Why?" Her questions slipped from her lips as she came to grips that Sal had a side of him that she didn't know and wished she still didn't.

"I was going under. The rent in the Plaza is not cheap. Delilah came by to clean, but I had to push her off for a couple weeks because I couldn't pay her. Then one day, she brought her son, Cody, and said he knew how to help me save the gallery. I couldn't pay him, but he agreed to work for free until the books changed around. I couldn't believe it when a month later I was in the black."

"And the drugs?" Bard asked. "When did you find out about those?"

"Last week." Sal looked at Natalie. "Honest. Natalie had been at the gallery when a man came in. He scared her, and when she came home, she told me what happened. I confronted Jemez and learned the truth."

"That he was selling drugs behind the paintings," Luci said. "That he had stuffed them with bricks of cocaine."

Sal's eyes widened and his mouth hung for a moment. "How did you know this? I don't understand why you're even here. You should be safe in your studio painting your next work."

Luci knew it was her time to come clean, no matter how it changed the way he saw her. Knowing this, didn't make it any easier to admit. She had no choice.

"The *Lady in Red.*"

"What about it?" Sal asked.

Luci frowned. "Three days ago, I was in the gallery, and I saw that it was marked with a sold card. But I had been coming in to take it back."

He squinted. "What for?"

She gnawed on her lower lip. "I had seen the real-life inspiration for the painting out in the Plaza the night before, and I realized I painted her eyes wrong. I gave her a sad look, but her eyes were not sad at all. They were wise. As if she knew something important." Luci took a deep breath and blurted, "So after hours, I went back to the gallery and took her back to fix her."

Sal jumped to his feet so fast that his chair went clattering to the floor. "You did what?" His voice raised so high that she cringed. He also caused Bard to bolt up, and before Sal could take one step toward her, Bard had a hand on the man's shoulder.

"You will lower your voice if you know what's good for you." Bard's voice was threaded with an unmistakable threat that had nothing to do with dangerous people outside and everything to do with him.

"But she caused this!" Sal shouted. "Natalie's been shot and Jemez is dead all because she took the painting?"

Bard turned the man and fisted his shirt in his hand. "No. *You* caused this when you allowed Cody Jemez to plant drugs in her paintings and smuggle them. Don't forget it started with you. And don't you ever accuse her of being the one at fault."

Sal pleaded, "I'm telling you, I didn't know."

Luci looked at Natalie. "What did the guy who took

my paintings look like? Do you have a name? Did he see you?"

Natalie shook her head. "I don't think so. I stayed low where I was cataloging some paintings. He didn't look friendly, and as soon as he left, I called Sal. I planned to call the police, but… Sal told me not to. And he told me to…forget what I saw."

Bard huffed again. "Convenient." He looked at Luci. "Do you want to change your opinion about this man yet?"

"No," she replied. "I trust that Sal had a valid reason for his decision." She looked at her mentor. "The man who came after me when I took the painting was going to kill me. Did you fear for your life as well?"

"Yes," Sal said. "But I didn't know what to do. I didn't know how to make them go away. I thought it best to just let them take your work. I told Jemez not to smuggle anymore. Honest. I told him I was done. I thought this would be the last one."

"Do you know who the man is? Do you know who the buyer is? This Fred Miller."

Sal shook his head. "That's the name Jemez wrote on the receipts. Miller paid cash. I have no way of tracking him."

Luci could see they had hit a dead end with Sal, but there was one thing she wanted to know, and this was her hardest question yet. "Do you know what he did with my paintings?"

"Oh, honey, I wish I did. But no, I do not." Sal looked so remorseful as Natalie grabbed her hand to squeeze.

"If we can find him, I can identify him," Natalie said with a little hope in her voice. "I would be happy to testify to put this man away."

Luci smiled at Nat, feeling so appreciative of this woman who had already been through so much at the hands of these evil people, especially with already being sick with cancer.

Sal picked up his chair and slumped down into it. "You're all forgetting something." With everyone's attention on him, he continued, "The name on all those paintings is Lucille Butler."

Luci leaned forward. "I don't understand. So what?"

Bard stepped away from Sal and back to the window. As he peered out from the side, he said, "He's telling you that you've been set up for drug smuggling. It's your name the feds will see, and it's you they'll come after." Bard put his gun up by his face, pointing it to the ceiling. With his eyes closed, he said quietly, "Not on my watch."

Bard knew that Luci could be wanted by both the organized criminal group and law enforcement. In fact, the feds could have all her paintings and already marked her as involved. So many of these smuggling operations had working undercover agents infiltrated, just waiting for the moment charges would stick before making their move. Ordinarily, he would be one of them. Knowing that the Bureau of Land Management's Santa Fe office was inundated with the constant flow of drugs coming up from the Mexican border only made him more worried for her future. The territory surrounding the forest acted as the perfect cover for aircraft to drop in and out of. The tributary rivers that led to the Rio Grande granted access for trafficking as well. All these details only solidified that they were not safe in this cabin.

"It's only a matter of time before we're surrounded," Bard told the silent group, still lost in their thoughts about how these paintings might lead to Luci. "We also need to find these paintings and get them back." He didn't want to think what he would do if he learned the feds already had them. Would he steal evidence that the government had confiscated?

"What's the plan?" Luci asked.

Sal stood and went over to a cabinet. "I have a map here somewhere. Perhaps you can get to the next ranger station before these guys return with more muscle."

Bard glanced out the window, not seeing any evidence of people in the trees. In fact, everything seemed tranquil. It was an idyllic location for a painter's retreat. But something didn't sit right with him. Bard thought of the man chasing Luci as she ran to this cabin. He had veered off just before she found it. He knew the guy was still out there, if not more of them by now.

But they kept their distance from this cabin.

Bard looked over at the table where Sal and Luci pored over the map.

"Take this route west and it will lead you to the next ranger station," Sal was instructing Luci. "You should make it by nightfall."

She put her hand down on the table over Sal's. "I want you to come with us. We can take turns carrying Natalie. You shouldn't be here. And she needs a doctor."

"The bullet went right through her leg. I got the bleeding to stop. I think any movement could start it again. Please don't worry about us. What's important is that you get to safety. I brought this on you, so please, get yourself to safety."

Tears welled up in Luci's eyes, shimmering them to a bright green. "I don't want you to feel guilty. I wish you hadn't resorted to crime to save the gallery, but please know I forgive you. What Cody Jemez did hurt us both. He took advantage of us and used us."

Sal pulled her close and rested his chin on top of her head. "I don't deserve your friendship."

You got that right, Bard thought. He checked himself, though, before saying anything not allowed. He was trying his hardest to give the man the benefit of the doubt when everything inside screamed that Sal was more guilty than he was letting on.

Bard scanned the room to take in the setup and art supplies. Paintings were displayed on every wall space, most not framed but in their raw canvas form. Three easels were stuffed into corners, with various projects in their early stages sitting on the ledges. Used painter's palettes were stacked on a side table by a floor-to-ceiling canvas mounted on the wall. The large mural was of a staircase going up into golden clouds. Bard studied Sal for a moment.

"Are you a praying man, Sal?" Bard asked.

The man flipped his hand back and forth. "Sometimes. Why do you ask?"

Bard nodded to the floor-to-ceiling canvas. "I was just wondering if that was a spiritual painting of some kind."

A strange look crossed the man's face. It only lasted for a second, but Bard caught it before it disappeared. The painting made him uncomfortable. And possibly even guilty.

"Nah, nothing spiritual," Sal said. "I think when I painted that, I was feeling a little low in my circumstances. It was more of a pep talk, that it was time to go up and claim what's mine."

"And what is that?" Bard stepped toward the canvas, crossing the small cabin's wood floor with slow thudding steps.

Sal shrugged as his eyes narrowed on Bard. "What any painter wants, I suppose. Fame, notoriety…make a living." Sal laughed a bit.

"Tough gig," Bard said, taking another step closer.

"That's why I opened the gallery. I thought if I could support other painters, I would get my piece of the gold at the same time."

"And yet here we are. Probably not how you envisioned taking your slice of the pie, correct?"

Sal frowned. He eyed the canvas, now only four feet away from Bard. "I said I was sorry. If I had known things would get this dangerous, I never would have hired Jemez. I would have let the gallery close and go under. But I can't go back. Now all I can do is protect my wife." He looked to Luci and took her hand. "And get you to safety."

Bard watched Luci's eyes fill with adoration for the man. "I want to thank you for believing in Luci's work," Bard said. "I think it's safe to say that you filled her with much needed hope." Bard took another step closer to the canvas.

Sal gazed down at Luci. "She's extremely talented. Surpasses me exponentially. I mean it, Luci. Don't let this situation deter you from your work. It does not reflect on the quality of your paintings in the least."

Bard nodded. "I'm glad to hear you say that. I think both of us wondered what you really thought."

Sal looked back at Bard. His eyes widened. "Before you both leave, I would like my gun back. It's all I have to protect Natalie."

Bard reached into the inside of his wet suit and took

out the revolver. "I can understand that. If you don't mind, I'll unload it first."

"That's fine." Sal swallowed so hard that his Adam's apple bounced.

Bard pushed out the side of the revolver and noticed the chambers were missing two bullets. He looked at the man over the gun, and as he removed the bullets, he said, "You really should keep this gun fully loaded. There are more than three bad guys out there."

"We were in a rush. That's all that was in the gun." Sal put out his hand for Bard to bring it over to him.

Instead, Bard took the last step to stand in front of the canvas. Bard wondered if those two bullets had ended up in Cody Jemez. The police had told him the man died from two fatal gunshots to the back. Would the bullets in Sal's revolver match the ones found in Jemez's body?

Once again, Bard chastised himself for jumping to conclusions. Sal's excuse of needing to run fast was valid. They hadn't even packed food to survive out here.

Bard put the revolver down on the side table with its many painter's palettes. The weapon juxtaposed with the symbol of creativity stirred resentment in him. He thought of Luci's studio going up in flames. Her whole life had been devoted to her art, and this man brought evil into her sanctuary.

With his eyes on Sal, Bard touched the middle of the canvas.

"You really shouldn't do that. The oils of your fingers can ruin it." Sal put a hand up to stop Bard. He moved to the end of the big table.

Bard knew he had mere seconds to figure out what this painting was doing here. He felt the whole cabin was a facade, and this time when he touched the canvas, he tapped on it three times.

Hollow.

There was nothing behind this painting, and when Bard reached for the edge to pull it away from the wall, Sal shouted for him to stop so loud that the windows shook and shattered.

Except, Bard realized that what was shattering the windows was a constant spray of bullets shooting the cabin up.

The relentless blasts shook the cabin and reverberated through his body as Bard dropped to the floor and raced over to Luci. He couldn't reach her fast enough, and when he finally touched her where she lay beneath the table, he felt blood on her arm.

A glance to his right, and he saw Natalie had already been killed. The woman slumped against the wall, never having the chance to even dodge her fatal shot.

All Bard could do was focus on Luci. He felt the slick wetness on her arm and hoped that's all that had touched her. He pulled her close and covered her as the bullets continued destroying everything around them. The hardwood table above them took the brunt of bullets that would have hit him, and when the eerie silence fell upon the cabin, Bard kept his head bent over hers for a few extra minutes.

He whispered, "We have to get out of here." Lifting his head, he scanned the cabin for Sal's body. There was no way the man survived that assault.

Except there was no sign of him anywhere. There was also no sign of Hero.

Staying low, Bard lifted his head higher to where the man had stood when the first shots had begun to fly. He had been running toward the canvas that was now lying on the floor where Hero had been. Bard looked up at the wall where the mural had been and saw a dark opening.

Crawling over, Bard saw quickly that it was a staircase, but instead of going up like the painting depicted, this one went down. Far down into the ground.

This cabin wasn't a painter's retreat. It was a stop on the drug smuggling route that just gave Sal a way out.

And apparently, Hero went after him.

THIRTEEN

Luci grabbed hold of her upper arm with her eyes scrunched in pain. She could feel blood seeping through her fingers and knew she had to stop the flow. Opening her eyes, she looked up to the underneath of the wooden table. Moments before, Bard had covered her, but he was gone now.

"Bard?" she spoke, but her throat clogged in pain. She moaned and turned her face to see him coming toward her on his belly. She got her first glimpse of the destroyed cabin and inhaled at the shocking site around her. Everything was obliterated. She kept her eyes on the man coming her way. "Where's Sal? Is he okay?"

Suddenly, Bard had her in his arms and pulled her close to him. "I need to get you out of here." She vaguely remembered him saying that only a little while ago, but he still hadn't answered her question.

"How? We'll be shot as soon as we step out of here."

"There's a stairway at the back. It's how Sal got out. Hero went with him."

"Stairway? I don't remember there being stairs." Her eyes dropped closed again in a searing pain that caught her breath. Then the second sentence registered. "Sal got out? What about Natalie?"

Bard glanced above Luci's head to look behind her. With a shake of his head, she had her answer. Instant tears welled up in Luci's eyes, but before she could let them spill, Bard grabbed her face and forced her to look at him. "There is nothing you can do for her now. All you can do is focus on staying alive. That is what she would want. To do anything else will only slow you down and get you killed. Do you understand?"

Luci sniffed and nodded. "But I'm bleeding a lot." She lifted a blood-soaked hand to show him. "It won't stop."

Bard scanned the room and then crawled over to the splintered cabinets. He pulled a towel from it, returned to her and then grabbed the map above them on the table. He passed them both to her for her to hold as he cradled her close to him and began to drag her across the floor. If she could walk, she would, but to stand up would be her death sentence. And with her wound, her arm was useless to help her crawl.

"I'm sorry if I'm hurting you," he said.

"I'm sorry for slowing you down."

He looked down at her. "Don't." They reached the halfway point between the table and the doorway to the stairs.

"How could I not? We're in this situation because I didn't let you do your job. I asked you to trust Sal. I feel like such a fool right now."

"Hold off your judgment of him until you have all the details." They reached the doorway, and he entered first to inspect below. Then he dragged her in and down the first couple of stairs.

She laughed a bit at the irony of his comment. "The man left his wife behind. That is all I need to know."

Bard paused beside her in the dark. She couldn't see his face clearly but felt him take her arm and tie the towel tightly around the wound.

"It's the best I can do right now. We have to keep going."

Luci looked below into the darkness. "What's down there?"

"I'm assuming a system of tunnels. I don't know where they'll take us, but Sal using them to flee tells me they lead to somewhere."

"For smuggling," she said, not needing any further explanation. "He knew these were here all along. Even when he brought me out here in the winter." Luci sighed. "How could I have been so wrong about him? And that explains why he gave me the loft and took the pullout sofa for him and Natalie." Luci inhaled sharply, looking back up the stairs. "Natalie had to have known too. I am such an idiot."

"No, you're not. And like I said. Just hold your judgment for now. I need you to focus on staying alive, and that's all I want you to think about right now."

This man had every right to tell her *I told you so*. But instead, he continued to worry about her safety and well-being. She leaned close to him and pressed her cheek to his. She felt let out a deep breath. They had never been this close to each other, but somehow, they had what the other needed to be able to think clearly.

As Bard's breathing slowed and his raging adrenaline evened out, he spoke in a whisper near her ear. "If anything happens to you, I think your brother will kill me." She felt his hand cup the back of her head as he turned her face to look at him. In the dimmest of light, all she could make out were the whites of his eyes. "And I will let him." She placed her hand on his chest, knowing it was guilt that drove him to protect her in the first place. She could not let that guilt drive him anymore.

"You're a good cop. And you always were." She dropped her head onto his forehead and took a deep breath. "What happens from this point on is not your fault. Now let's get out of here. We need to find Hero."

Bard pulled away but she could still feel his warm breath on her cheek. After a moment, he whispered, "You are a treasure, Luci Butler." He leaned close and placed a soft kiss on her cheek. It wasn't anything romantic, but rather a moment to remind them that they were still alive, and they could do this.

In the next second, he left her and disappeared into the dark. Just when her heart picked up in anxiety, he returned.

"Can you stand?" he asked.

Luci stood, and he wrapped an arm around her waist, careful to hold her from the other side of her injured arm. "I can walk fine. You don't have to hold me up."

He huffed a little laugh in her hair. "I can't believe I'm going to admit this, but I think it might be *you* holding *me* up right now."

She scoffed at the absurdity of that statement. This giant of a man needing her made no sense. But then she thought of that constant barrage of bullets. "I'm not even sure how this cabin is standing anymore."

Bard made a low whistle and then stood quietly beside her. She knew he was hoping his dog would hear and come back. He looked behind them and then in front. "I don't know the direction Sal would have gone."

"Wouldn't Hero catch him?" As soon as she asked

that question, she could tell what was really bothering Bard. He was worried his dog had been injured… or worse.

Hero might have been shot, and even with an injury, he went after Sal. Would Sal hurt him further? Only moments before the shooting, she would have said no. Sal could never hurt anyone. Now she couldn't say any such thing. And if Bard lost his dog over her misplaced trust of the man, she would never forgive herself.

When nothing but silence surrounded them, it was obvious that Hero wasn't coming back, and Luci felt the weight of that guilt bending her head down.

She never dreamed taking that painting off the wall would lead to all of this. But they couldn't go back now. They could only move forward.

Even if forward was pitch-black and into an evil crime ring that wanted her dead.

Bard turned an ear to above the stairs and could hear footsteps crunching through the debris. He couldn't wait any longer to get Luci out of there. He had hoped Hero would return after his whistle, but the dog must have been too far away. Bard hoped that's all it was, and that he would run across him at some point.

As he guided Luci step-by-step through the narrow space, he kept one arm around her waist and one hand on the wall of dirt. He felt brackets along the way that held the earth above at bay, and at some point, the ground and walls became wet.

"I hear dripping," Luci whispered.

Bard hesitated to give his opinion, but he needed her to walk swiftly. "We're under the river. We have to move fast."

She picked up her steps along with him, but the gravity of the situation kept them both silent until finally the earth around them dried up.

She gave a little nervous laugh and said, "Can I just admit that that was a little easier than the rapids?"

"And a lot less visual, which is why the smugglers dug underground."

"I guess I always knew there were people out in the world that lived lives like this, but I never gave their operations much thought." She spoke low with an understanding of the danger they were in. "The fact that they can be so evil when one person disrupts their system makes me wonder how many lives have been lost at their hands."

"Too many to count," Bard responded solemnly. "Law enforcement does their best to curtail it, but they barely make a dent. We're more of a hindrance than a threat to them. Still, we show up the next day and be the best thorn in their side that we can be."

"Do you ever fear for your life?"

Bard took a moment to think about his answer. They walked on for what seemed like miles, but the fact that they were moving so slow, it probably wasn't that long of a distance. They came to more soggy dirt, and Bard figured they were going back under the river again. He wondered how long the stops were in between in this well-designed labyrinth beneath the national forest.

"I can't say I fear for my life," he finally answered. "That's a risk I accepted when I took the job. If I have one main concern that could be considered a fear, I would say it would be letting down the people who trust me to get these bad guys behind bars before they hurt more people."

He heard her sigh in the dark. "And I made you do that."

"I let you. Don't take that guilt on yourself. I didn't have to listen to you."

"Then why did you?" She stopped, and his arm began to slip from her back before he did as well. "Do you feel that guilty about letting my brother down that you would trust a young, naive starving painter who knows nothing about this smuggling world?"

Bard smiled. "Well, when you put it like that, I suppose I should have been a little tougher on you. Maybe I felt a little bad for you."

"Bad for me? For what?" She pulled farther away from him, and he dropped his hand to his side.

"Oh, I don't know, maybe it was when you asked me to pack your measly belongings so they wouldn't burn in the fire that did it for me. I thought you deserved so much more than a small box of belongings to represent your life. Or maybe it was when we went to visit your parents and I saw you suffocating in their presence. I felt the need to demand they apologize to you. How could they ever think you are invisible? Or perhaps it was the moment when I first laid eyes on you and watched you steal a painting right off the gallery wall. I saw firsthand how crime isn't always black and white. I left my post in Carlsbad because I was doubting my capabilities to be a fair and just investigator. And then you came along—this little pixie of a thing who was bold and brave, but most of all, compassionate—and you showed me what I was missing. I had the bold and brave parts down, but I'm thoroughly lacking in the compassion area. But not you. I find your heart for people to be one of the most beautiful and comforting things about you.

And that's saying a lot since you're stunning. Don't tell your brother I said that."

Bard trailed off as he realized he was spilling his guts in the darkness, and he wasn't even sure if she was still there. He reached out and only touched air. It was probably just as well she wasn't.

"Luci?" He spoke into the dark.

And then she was there, back in front of him, placing her hand on his chest over his wet suit. She moved it up to his throat and came along the side of his cheek.

"You're too tall."

"For what?" he asked as he brought his hand around her lower back. He liked holding her there. There was something comforting about being able to touch her that lessened his anxiety, and maybe even his loneliness.

"To kiss you." Her bold words parched his throat in an instant. He glanced down to where he knew she only came to the middle of his chest. With the fingers of his free hand, he reached for the side of her face, feeling his way to lift her chin and lips to his.

Bard used his hand at her back to lift her up and bent his knees to meet her halfway. But just before he lowered his lips to hers, he said, "Is this better?"

She spoke in a whisper. "It's perfect." She pulled his head down and captured his lips for the sweetest connection he had ever experienced. This little bundle in his arms filled him with joy even in a moment that could be their last. He had told her he didn't fear death, but suddenly, he realized he feared something else.

Bard felt his heart clench in his chest as he kissed Luci and knew he was crossing the line. In his whole career, his mind had been his greatest asset. His knowledge and strength came from his ability to analyze and weed out the good from the bad. But with Luci, she challenged him to think with his heart instead.

And that could be more dangerous than any bad guy he'd ever chased.

Bard pulled away and lowered her back to the ground. He felt her turn her cheek to his chest and rest there for a moment. He knew he should push her away, but he needed the time to gain his footing. With his hand at her back, he felt her tremble, and he felt her wrap her arms around him. For her own safety, he should move away. He would be no good to her if he did not keep a level head and work from where he was skilled. She may have worked from her heart, but he couldn't.

With more strength than he thought he had in him, he stepped out of her grasp and let his hand fall from her back. "We have to keep going. That shouldn't have happened," he said, hearing the harshness in his voice. He cringed at the sound but resolved that it was for the best.

"I see," Luci said, the irony being he didn't need to turn on the lights for her to understand.

She took the first steps and he followed close behind her. When he heard her trip twice, he wanted to reach out and help her, but she pushed his hand away.

"I need to protect you," he said. "That's all I can focus on. Please understand."

"It's fine," she said quickly. "It won't happen again. Promise."

The finality in her voice felt like a sucker punch. But he deserved it. He couldn't offer her anything than what he already had. "I came to Santa Fe to protect you. I owed it to—"

She halted. "If you even say my brother one more time, I give you permission to leave and never come back. I didn't ask you to come and neither did he. If that's the only reason why you're here, then go."

She sounded six feet tall. So much so that he straightened to his full height. "Your brother just faced one of the most lethal criminal families in the world with the patriarch still at large. I thought it best to alert his family. I hate to think what would have happened to you if I hadn't acted on that decision, even if this smuggling ring has nothing to do with the Lindsay crime family. This is what I mean when I say I have to focus. I can stay two steps ahead of the bad guys when I use my mind. But with you, Luci, all reasoning escapes me. I'm watching your life be put at risk at every turn, and all I can think is if I just acted on what I knew, all of this wouldn't have happened. We wouldn't be standing in a drug tunnel beneath a vast forest in the pitch-dark with no direction."

"So it's my fault. Fine. I get it." She turned to walk away from him.

Bard reached out a hand and quickly grasped hers to stop her. "No. It's *my* fault. You're not understanding me."

"Then help me understand why kissing me is so revolting."

Bard sputtered before he could control his laugh. He wished he could see her face, but it was probably best that she couldn't see his. As he looked to the ceiling and pleaded with God for help, he knew all he could do was be honest. "You make me want to be a better person. You make me want to be more compassionate." He swallowed hard, never feeling so vulnerable. "You asked me what I'm afraid of? That's it. If I don't stay focused, I fear you won't make it out of this alive. That's what I'm afraid of. Up above, out in the woods, I expected to find your dead body around every turn. When that shoot-out occurred upstairs in the cabin, I couldn't get to you. Those are the things that I find revolting. Kissing you was not revolting. No. In fact, it was so amazing that I realized the danger we would be in—*you* would be in if I let it go any further. Because I realized I was acting from my heart and not my head. I don't know what I'm doing from that place. And I fear I'll fail you if I stay there."

He could feel her tension decrease through her hand. "Okay. I appreciate you sharing that. I'm sure it wasn't easy." She pulled her hand from his. In the next second, she turned back and said, "I found another staircase."

Bard moved to full alert. "Right here?" He walked around her, and sure enough, another set of wooden stairs like the ones to Sal's cabin went up from the right. "Walk up with me, but I want you waiting until I say it's safe to come in."

Suddenly, a bark came from above. He would know that sound anywhere. And before he could stop her, Luci ran up the stairs with him. He put his hand out to stop her from going farther, but as they reached the door and pushed through, light flooded into the stairwell, revealing an empty room.

Then all Bard heard was Luci inhale on a sharp gasp.

FOURTEEN

Luci stared at what used to be the painting of her favorite hot-air balloon at Albuquerque's balloon festival. She had captured the vibrant colors glinting off the rays of the sunrise coming up over the canyon. She remembered that morning and how she had to paint the scene from memory because the balloon drifted over her and out of the light so quickly. She had been so proud of it when it was finished, but not nearly as proud as when it sold.

Luci stepped into the room—another run-down cabin but larger than Sal's. She moved closer to the mangled and torn canvas that had been tossed to the side once the drugs inside were removed. She saw her name scrawled on the bottom right corner and turned away from the disappointing sight.

"Are there any more?" she asked Bard. "I can't look."

As she faced his shoulder, he looked over her head and around the room. "Just a bunch of busted frames. I don't see any more paintings, but that doesn't mean they hadn't been here. I'm sorry. I'll do my best to get them back. We have to with your name on them. But right now, we need to go through that closed door and figure out where we are. And get my dog." Bard sounded angrier than she had heard him yet.

He had removed his gun from inside his wet suit and now pointed it at the door.

Luci followed behind him as he stepped slowly and treaded lightly along the floorboards. He jerked his head to the right to have her move closer to the corner of the room. They had no idea if anyone was even in the house with them. If they had Hero, they most likely were expecting them.

Hero barked again and could be heard butting up against something hard, like another door in the cabin.

Bard turned the knob and pushed the door in, quickly moving to the side with his gun ready to shoot. The dog's barking grew louder, and all Luci could see was Bard scanning the room before he moved inside. She heard him open another door, and Hero barked louder.

"It's empty. Of people anyway. Come in here," he instructed her.

Luci entered the room and saw Hero exiting a bathroom. She also noticed the one window in the room had been painted black, so she couldn't see outside. Then she saw their backpacks.

"They have our things." She spoke low as she made her way over to the two bags. When she reached hers, she glanced back to see Bard looking around the room.

"I don't see any cameras, but that doesn't mean they're not hidden in the lights or a hole in the wall." He stepped up to a small bathroom with just a toilet and sink. "Go ahead and get changed." He bent down and checked his dog all over.

"Is he hurt?" Luci asked while she pulled out a pair

of black pants and a running shirt. It would feel good to be back in real clothes.

"His eyes are weird. They might have knocked him out with something. It would explain why he didn't run back."

"You're being kind. If anyone knocked him out, it would be Sal."

He didn't deny it, and she took the clothes and went inside the bathroom to quickly change.

When Luci returned, Bard had already changed as well. He was back in his tan tactical pants and black shirt. As she emerged, he was in the process of lacing up his boots. He tossed her a pair of sneakers, and she quickly donned them.

"Now what?" she asked.

"I don't think we have a choice. They know we're here. I would say they're waiting right outside for us."

Luci looked back at the room with her painting. "Should we go back to the tunnel?"

"I feel that would be more dangerous."

She looked at the bags. "Is the satellite radio still in there?"

"No. They took it. Along with the drugs."

"So if they have what they want, maybe they'll let us go." She knew it was wishful thinking. The fact was they were cornered. No matter what direction they went, these men would be ready to stop them.

"They want the painting. They haven't asked for the drugs."

She glanced at the hot-air balloon massacred in the other room. "It makes no sense. They just destroy them. Why would they need my *Lady in Red* if that's all they're going to do with it?"

Suddenly, overhead, the whomping sound of a helicopter's blades drew near, growing louder as it passed over and landed someplace close by.

"Sounds like we have company," Bard said. To Hero, he said, "Guard."

The K-9 stepped up to Luci and took his position. She reached down and touched his thick brown coat. He tensed as his muscles rippled. She didn't doubt that he would offer his life to protect her.

In the next second, the door burst open, and Bard shouted, "Drop your weapons or I'll shoot!"

Luci shouted, "Stop! Don't shoot!"

Sal stood in the doorway with two other men.

"They're my brothers," she said, running into Tru's open arms.

"Tru," Bard said in confusion. "What are you doing here?"

Tru sent a scathing look at Bard from over Luci's head. "I could ask you the same thing."

"What is this place, Sal?" Bard ignored Tru's question and gave his full attention to the traitorous man. Bard questioned the sting of jealousy percolating at the sight of Luci being rescued by these two capable men. He should have been happy she would get out of this place. He had a job to do, and the best thing would be for her to be taken out of here.

But he wanted to be the one to get her to safety, not Sal.

Sal answered, "It's exactly what it looks like, but I'm trying to make this right for Luci. Tru contacted me when Luci wasn't answering her phone."

Tru said, "I was calling all your friends that I could

think of, just hoping someone would know where you were."

Sal continued, "Once I got to this cabin and got his message, I called him back right away and told him to come here. I really never meant for her to be involved." Sal looked to Luci. "Please, you have to believe me. Go with your brothers and get out of here while you can."

It took every ounce of strength not to pummel the lying man to the floor. Bard couldn't fathom what he'd just been told. Sal was here with Luci's brothers. The whole scene didn't mesh. Were her siblings involved somehow? Bard felt for his handcuffs in one of the pockets. He only had one pair, not that Luci would let him arrest any of them. It had never been so hard to do his job. They all looked guilty from his point of view, and he had to force himself to think differently about them.

"What about you?" she asked Sal, stepping closer to him.

Bard could already see she was softening toward the man. She would give him another chance to explain himself. Couldn't she see the man was a liar? He obviously knew more than he told her. He knew about these tunnels. He knew about this cabin.

Sal replied, "I have to go back for Natalie. Don't worry about me. Please, just go."

"I'm not worried about you anymore. Tell me why I should let you get away with this? Your wife is dead. Cody Jemez is dead. You have caused these horrible things, all because you wanted to save your business? You are despicable. Did you hit Hero to knock him out?"

Bard glanced her way. Had he heard her right? Was she holding the man accountable? Did she finally see the truth about this man she called a friend?

Bard felt for his handcuffs again but knew they weren't there. Whoever went through the bags had emptied his pockets. But he didn't let on that he was without resources. "Not to mention Luci's still not safe. I don't care if you called her brothers. I don't care how helpful you have been to her. You belong behind bars, and you can be sure, I will see that you are found and taken in."

"Bard, what do you really want to do?" Luci asked, drilling him with those intense green eyes. "What would you do in this moment if I hadn't asked you to change?"

Bard studied her face to see if she was serious. He'd never seen her look so sure. She stood with her legs braced in strength, and her hands were on her hips. She looked to the back of Sal's head and sneered.

Suddenly, Bard felt bad for the man. Luci's visible disdain was lethal. If he had thought she was weak when it came to her support of Sal, Bard could now see she could be just as determined to see him go down.

"Are you sure?" he asked.

"Cuff him." Her response nearly caused him to crack a smile. This is what he lived for. Taking down the bad guys, and Sal Ramon was the worst. He preyed on young unsuspecting women, telling them what they wanted to hear to get their loyalty, and then used them.

Even putting them into danger.

Bard looked to Tru. "Do you have your handcuffs on you?"

An expression of uncertainty crossed his friend's face. Tru replied, "Yes, but Sal called us. He gave us the coordinates to this place. Why would he do that if he's as guilty as you think? This wouldn't be the first time you were wrong about a suspect, Bard. Do I need to remind you how you wanted to arrest Danika?"

Luci turned back to face her brother. "Bard is right. Sal is scum. I'm sorry that happened to you, Tru, but Bard knows what he's doing, and one slip doesn't change that. We have to let him do his job now. I shouldn't have stopped him in the first place." She looked at Sal again with such anger. "That's something I'll regret for the rest of my life, but not nearly as much as ever befriending you."

Sal frowned and reached a hand to Luci. That's when Bard noticed the teeth marks on his forearm. As Sal's hand came forward, the cuff of his shirt lifted just enough for Bard to see the fresh wounds.

Bard reached out and snatched the hand before he touched Luci. "I see Hero *did* get to you." Bard's blood began to boil. He wanted to know what the man had done to his dog, but he thought it best not to ask. The truth might have pushed him over the edge. If Bard wanted to make this arrest stick, he needed to do everything by the book. That meant keeping a level head.

He twisted the man's hand up from behind him and turned him around. Bard looked to Tru for the handcuffs.

Luci's brother still hesitated.

"I'm sorry for failing you as a cop and as your friend," Bard said. "But please, trust me. This man is dirty."

Tru looked to his brother. Jett Butler shrugged but said, "I don't know the situation, but this operation looks bigger than any of us, including Sal. Guilty or not, he might be safer in custody."

Sal shook his head. "I'm a dead man no matter what you do. They'll get to me anywhere."

Tru asked, "Who is *they*? Help us out, and maybe things will go easier for you."

"I really don't know. Honest. I told Luci the truth about Jemez bringing this group to my doorstep."

Bard said, "Jemez died of two gunshot wounds that I think came from your revolver. Did you kill him?"

Sal dropped his gaze to the floor and didn't respond.

In the next second, Tru pressed his lips tight and handed over the handcuffs to Bard without any more hesitancy. But just as Bard clicked them into place, the front door blasted open, and the window to Bard's left smashed in. Suddenly, they were surrounded by federal agents with guns drawn on them all. A sea of FBI, DEA and BLM agents swarmed them, all dressed in identifying jackets and protective gear.

"Hands behind your heads! All of you!" one of the agents who came through the front door yelled.

Bard followed orders as he said, "I'm a BLM investigator." Although he doubted his badge was still in the backpack.

Hero barked ferociously as three of the agents held him down and kept him from guarding Luci as he had been commanded. Bard moved to help his dog, but then saw as Luci was thrust to the floor face-first. The agent handcuffed her with no concern of hurting her.

"Lucille Butler, you are under arrest for drug smuggling."

Bard reached his hands out to stop them. "Go easy on her! Be careful of her arm. She was shot! She's innocent in all this. She's been set up. Let me take her in."

The agent picked her up like a rag doll and pushed her toward the front door. "You had your chance. You caught her in the act with possession of illegal drugs.

If you're a federal agent, then you should know that deciding her innocence isn't your job. That's for the judge and jury. Our job depends on the evidence, and we have all the evidence we need."

Bard's last glimpse of Luci was the fearful look in her widened green eyes that moments ago had been filled with so much strength. Now she resembled the girl he originally saw her as, and there was nothing he could do to help her anymore.

FIFTEEN

The federal agents didn't have to push Luci's head down as they stuffed her in the back of their unmarked car. She hung her head in shock and remorse. The men handled her as though she was the vilest of offenders and didn't deserve any semblance of care. They considered her to be a part of this heinous operation and no different than Sal. Their treatment of her shocked her, but her remorse had nothing to do with guilt and everything to do with trusting the wrong man.

She glanced out her side window and saw another black federal car with Sal in the back seat. She had trusted this man with her deepest secrets and everything she held dear. She'd latched on to his every word and swallowed every piece of advice, letting him guide her in her craft and in her business. She'd considered him the only real family she'd had in twelve years. When no one else had time for her, he gave her his every waking moment and never made her feel needy or unwanted.

It had all been a lie.

All she had wanted was to be noticed, and the only reason why he noticed her was to take advantage of her and use her.

The handcuffs cut into her wrists, and she adjusted her position to release some weight on them. "You mentioned you had evidence?" she asked the man behind the steering wheel.

He didn't even turn back to look at her.

Before putting her in the car, he had read out her rights. She knew speaking could be held against her, but she had to know what kind of evidence they had on her. The only thing she was guilty of was being too invested in her paintings.

Her paintings. That had to be the only thing they had on her. Which meant they had them.

"Are they ruined? Were my paintings destroyed by the smugglers? Please, I have to know." She knew she sounded desperate, but this was her first glimpse of hope at finding some of them. "Are any of them salvageable?"

A second agent climbed into the passenger seat and looked back at her. He sneered as if he hated her. Knowing Bard always got his bad guy, she wondered if he ever looked at them in the same hurtful manner. She couldn't imagine him being so cruel. Even if the perpetrator was a hundred percent guilty. Bard had a level of integrity that these men lacked.

"All I want to know is if you have my paintings," she said. She heard her voice trembling, but she wouldn't let her fear deter her.

"All but one. And I don't mean the one we just grabbed from inside."

She knew he could only be talking about her *Lady in Red*. She thought of where she hid it in the gallery and nearly told them where they'd find it.

The look of hatred on his face stopped her. Why should she offer up evidence that would only incriminate her further? *Let them do their own work*, she thought.

The driver started the engine and pulled out of the secluded area so fast that she hit the back of her head on the seat. More rough and careless treatment toward her only solidified her resolve to say nothing more to them. She turned back and saw her brothers and Bard by her brother's rescue chopper. Jett was head of search and rescue on the mountain in Taos and had his own SAR helicopter. He rescued people for his living, but she had to admit she was surprised he had come for her.

It had been twelve years since his car accident, but he only started remembering everyone in the last two years. The way he avoided her made her wonder if he remembered her at all. There was such an age gap between them, and when she was fourteen, he was too busy dating Nikki and building a home for them after their wedding. The accident tore them apart until two years ago. Luci was glad he and Nikki had found each other again, but it still hurt to not have a connection with her oldest brother. Luci could only reason that Tru had called Jett, told him the circumstances and convinced him to come with his helicopter. Had they told their parents? For the briefest of moments, Luci wondered what her arrest would do to her parents' already fragile relationship.

As the car drove her to her unknown future, she laid her head back and closed her eyes and prayed for God to intervene. *God? How did I end up here? Tell me what You want me to do.*

The silence that followed made her wonder if she was even invisible to Him.

She opened her eyes to see the man in the passenger

seat texting someone. But before he hit Send, she saw it said, we got her. the rest are following.

The rest?

As far as she saw back there, Sal was the only other one arrested. She saw her brothers and Bard by the helicopter, free to go.

Luci turned her ear to the sound of Jett's helicopter off in the distance. She noticed that it didn't grow distant but stayed constant. As though Jett was following them.

The rest are following. The text began to make sense.

"What's going on?" she asked even though she knew they wouldn't respond. She leaned forward. "Something's not right. I know I've never been in this situation before, but I know something's wrong with all of this."

"Just sit back and relax," the driver said, looking at her through the rearview mirror. "It will all be over soon."

Over? What was that supposed to mean? The weight of the realization hit her like another bullet.

These were not federal agents.

These were the drug smugglers posing as agents.

Luci twisted around to find the car with Sal was no longer behind them. The only thing behind her was her brother's helicopter with both her brothers and Bard aboard.

"Have I been kidnapped?"

The driver chuckled. "You were right," he said to the passenger beside him. "She's quick."

With all her might, Luci kicked at the door, straining for leverage with her hands cuffed behind her. She felt her gunshot wound begin to seep again from the pressure. If she bled out while she tried to kick out, so be it. She couldn't let these men take her to whatever location they had in mind.

The chopper grew closer.

She also didn't want her brothers and Bard to be ambushed.

She kicked harder, but it was no use. The door wouldn't budge. Panic threatened her clear thinking. She couldn't let it overcome her. She was quick on her feet, but first she had to get out of this car.

She had to alert the men above that she'd been kidnapped.

But how?

She couldn't wave and shouting would do nothing. All she had *were* her feet.

Luci leaned back on her arms, biting through the pain the cuffs and her bullet wound caused. With all her might, she bent her knees and kicked at the glass. Twice nothing happened. With all her strength, she pulled from deep within her the loudest growl and used it for a third kick with both her feet smashing through the glass and out the window.

It wasn't perfect, and the glass cut her legs, but she knew it worked when the helicopter grew a bit distant.

The passenger turned and reached over the back to grab her and pull her back in, slicing her further. The pain was searing but knowing her brothers and Bard wouldn't follow her to their demise made it all worth it.

"You're gonna regret that," her kidnapper sneered. "Wait until the boss hears about this."

Luci rolled over in pain but lifted her head and looked right at him. "Take me to him, so I can tell him about it myself."

In the next second, the man raised his beefy fist and brought it down over her head, spiraling her into darkness.

* * *

"Why did she kick out the glass?" Bard asked through his headset in the helicopter. Didn't she know that would be considered resisting arrest?

Jett responded, "That's what it looked like to me. Something's wrong. I'm holding back for a moment."

"Don't lose her! Please, don't lose her!" Bard sat in the back with Hero beside him. The two Butler brothers sat up front, and judging by the look Tru just sent him, they were both wondering what Luci was to him.

He had no answer for them.

As Bard looked out the window to keep track of the direction of the car, he asked himself what *was* Luci to him?

She was his challenger, that much he knew. She made him question his actions, but at the same time she respected his job. The federal agents may have told him he failed his job by not taking her in, but he knew if he had, then he wouldn't have found the true bad guys. She showed him that sometimes the most obvious solution wasn't the correct one. Sometimes the most obvious solution was the easy way out.

"Tru?" He spoke quietly into the microphone, and when his friend turned back to him, all he could say was, "I'm sorry. What I did to you and Danika was a cop-out. I know in my laziness, I caused serious damage. I brought more danger to you both, and I ruined our friendship. I know you almost lost her because of me and my choice to look no further for the true criminal."

Tru nodded and looked at his brother, then back at Bard. "I'd say that the fact that you didn't take Luci in right away tells me you learned your lesson. You dug deeper even when common sense said she was guilty. We thank you for that." He closed his eyes for a moment and pressed his lips. When he looked at Bard again, he said, "I've been given a second chance, and it would be wrong of me not to do the same for you. Consider it forgotten, friend." Tru faced forward. "We need to focus on getting her out of these charges. And we're going to need you."

Bard looked out the window for the federal vehicle. "You can count on it. I won't be leaving her side. I should've fought to go in the car with her."

Tru glanced back at him again with that same expression of wondering what Luci was to him. Bard didn't think it was the time to lie to his friend. After just being forgiven, Bard thought honesty would be the best route to take.

"I care about your sister. A lot."

Tru's eyes widened as Hero lifted his head. Having the declaration out there for everyone to hear was liberating.

"Your sister is like no one I've ever met. You always made her sound like your annoying baby sister, but I have to think you've been missing out on knowing an amazing, strong woman. I think your whole family is missing out, and if I can speak honestly, she's felt the rejection from you all."

Tru narrowed his eyes and looked about ready to take back his forgiveness. But before he said anything, Jett cut in.

"It's my fault," he said.

Tru looked to his brother. "No. What happened to

you was an accident and nobody's fault. We have you back now, and you can't carry this guilt any longer."

"But we also can't ignore the fact that Luci got lost along the way. It's time we bring her home, where she belongs." Jett blew out a deep breath into the microphone. He lifted his head to ask Bard, "Does she return the same feelings that you have for her?"

Before Bard could say he wasn't sure, he thought of her kiss in the tunnel...and at his apartment. A quick smile cracked his lips as he realized she had lifted her face to him when he only meant to kiss her forehead. The kiss on her lips hadn't been an accident at all. The little pixie was quick, that was for sure. He had thought he'd slipped up and had even told her he wasn't sorry. She sure was a woman of many secrets and talents.

Tru looked at Bard. "I'll take that as a yes." The two brothers sent each other concerned expressions.

Bard leaned forward. "I can't speak for her, but I want you to know, it wasn't anything we planned. I'm sure nothing will come of it when we all go back to our normal lives. And I promise you, she will get her life back. These charges won't stick. I'll make sure the whole truth is known."

"Except, if you two are a couple, no one will believe anything you say if it protects her," Tru said. "Your testimony is useless."

Bard felt as if Tru just punched him.

"Guys?" Jett interrupted Bard's spiraling thoughts. "The car is not heading toward the interstate. It's not leaving the federal property at all. It just took a turn onto a nonaccess road and disappeared into the trees."

Bard went back to the window and couldn't see the car anymore. Panic set in. He knew something felt wrong. Luci wasn't resisting arrest when she kicked the window out.

She was trying to escape with her hands cuffed.

"Find that car!" he shouted. "Those weren't agents. Those were the criminals, and now they have her!"

SIXTEEN

Luci groaned as the seat beneath her head bounced her up and down. She opened her eyes, but pain shot to her head, so she closed them quickly. She was still in the car with the men who kidnapped her, and they were obviously off-road, driving over some rough terrain.

"Tell the boss we're almost there," one of the men said. *It's the driver*, she thought.

"Just did. He's eager to meet the chick. Says she made this all too easy." That was definitely the passenger kidnapper.

Luci pushed past the pain to turn an ear to the conversation. She remained in her prostrate position to let the men think she was still unconscious.

"What are we getting paid for this job? Do you know?"

"I'm told we'll be set for years."

"Nice. I've got my eye on a little hacienda downtown."

The passenger laughed. "Aren't you the little homemaker. Since when have you wanted to become a homeowner?"

"Everyone needs a place to lay their head. I'm done with motel living. Besides, Rita's asking too many questions about where my money's coming from. This will shut her up."

"True that. She better be careful, or she'll be shut up…for good."

"I've told her, but you know women. Sometimes they go too far."

"Like this chica in the back. Busting my window was too far. I'm looking forward to making her pay by busting something of hers. Like her knees. Or maybe those bony fingers of hers. One snap at a time." The guy laughed in a sick and twisted way.

Luci swallowed so hard she was sure they heard her gulp. She didn't dare open her eyes to find out; just held her breath and prayed they would continue to think she was unconscious. Maybe as long as she was out, they would wait to break her bones.

"Will Lindsay be here?"

"Supposed to be. With the cash."

"Perfect."

The two quieted down as they drove on, but Luci's mind strained to figure out who was Lindsay? Should she know this woman in some way? Had she wronged Lindsay in the past? For the woman to go to these extremes to set her up for drug smuggling and kidnap her, Luci had to think their paths had crossed before.

The name seemed vaguely familiar, but she couldn't place the reason why. She couldn't remember ever meeting anyone named Lindsay. Perhaps at one of the gallery events?

That had to be it. And how Luci's paintings became the chosen pieces for the smuggling operation. Lindsay must have been a regular at the gallery.

As the idea grew from speculative to probable, Luci's

heart rate raced. She had to be getting closer to figuring out who was behind this whole setup. More than anything she wanted to ask questions, but supposedly being unconscious was the only thing saving her life at the moment. Saving her life had to be her number one priority. The identity of Lindsay would have to wait.

"Do you think we'll get paid if we don't have the last painting?" the driver asked, perking Luci's ears back to their conversation. "I don't know what the big deal is. The chick's a nobody."

"Oh, and now you're some sort of connoisseur of art, are you?"

The driver laughed. "That's a big word for you. Can you spell it?"

The passenger replied, "How about I just shoot you instead?"

Luci held her breath until finally both men laughed. Although, the driver's laugh seemed a little forced. She wondered if perhaps the man who was looking to settle down and buy a house just might be a lifeline for her. She didn't dare trust either of them, but perhaps the driver could be persuaded to come to the other side.

But then, money talks, and this Lindsay woman sounded like she's loaded. How would Luci compete with her promise of enough money for a house? She was homeless herself. She had nothing to offer him.

Nothing but…the *Lady in Red*.

Maybe Luci could promise him the painting and convince him to get her out of there to get it. Then he could claim to be the one to track it down and get the whole load Lindsay promised them. He could buy two houses with all that money by the sound of it. He could just explain that Luci got away, or he killed her…without actually killing her, of course.

A bit of queasiness came over her. It could have been the jostling of the car, but it could also have been the fact that she was plotting to conspire with murderers and drug smugglers.

But what other choice did she have? Death was inevitable…and apparently so were broken bones.

The deafening silence inside Bard's headphones was louder than the whomping of the helicopter blades above him. No one inside could say a word until they found the car again; all lost in their fears.

Jett hovered over the thick forest with no direction, and Bard could see how this area made for a prime location for drug trafficking. It's no wonder the law barely made a dent. The criminals had ample cover and could go undetected before anyone knew they had even been there. Why hadn't he thought about that when they supposedly raided the cabin and took Luci and Sal away.

Suddenly, Bard had an idea.

"What happened to Sal's car?"

Jett replied, "It veered off a while back. I just figured they were taking him to a different location, being that he was considered dangerous."

"Except now we know these weren't feds. Can you find it again?"

Jett lifted up higher and turned back. "Are you sure about this? I think we should stay in the vicinity of Luci."

"I think they want us to do just that. They're luring us for some reason."

"Then why lose us?"

"Because they know we'll stay there looking for her, and they'll know where to find us."

"And do what?"

Before Bard could respond to Jett's question, the helicopter jolted and tipped.

Jett struggled at the controls, but his fast reflexes righted the aircraft quickly.

Until the chopper took another hit.

"We're being shot at!" Jett yelled, lifting higher and swinging out. The helicopter jolted again; this time being sent into a tailspin. "I have to get out of here, but they won't let me!"

Multiple bullets pelted them from all directions.

"It's an ambush!" Tru yelled. The glass in front of him fractured.

Hero barked uncontrollably beside Bard. No amount of comforting him and covering him eased his hysterics. Not that Bard could blame him. In any second, a bullet could hit the gas and blow them all to pieces. He wanted to yell as well, but that would only cause Jett more stress. The man knew how to handle his helicopter better than anyone, and no matter what happened, he did his best.

"I have to take her down," Jett said in an apologetic voice. "I'm leaking fuel."

Tru responded, "But where?"

Jett leaned over to his left. "There's a small opening over here. It's our only hope."

"You do realize that this is exactly what they wanted, right?" Bard said.

The two brothers looked at each other. Tru glanced

back at Bard and nodded. "We're heading right into danger. You have your gun ready?"

Bard took it out of his back waistband to show Tru. "It's nothing to what they have down there, but yeah, I have it."

Jett said, "In the bag behind me are two rifles. I want you both taking one."

Bard leaned forward. "What about you?"

In the next second, Jett lifted his left hand and showed it covered with blood. "I've been compromised. I've lost all feeling in my arm and won't be able to handle it. My handgun will be all I can shoot."

"We'll cover you," Bard promised. He looked at Tru and said, "If I didn't know any better, I'd say these people are targeting the Butler family. They also most likely got Sal to lead you both here to take you out. Stay alert."

Tru's face grew ashen. His eyes grew wide as he spoke. "Lindsay?"

Bard nodded. "It crossed my mind. But right now, who's behind this doesn't matter. Finding Luci alive does."

The blades of the helicopter sputtered above him, and as Jett lowered them into the small clearing, they brushed against the tops of the trees, free-falling the last few feet before the chopper's runners smacked hard against the ground.

All three men groaned with the jarring impact, but knew every second was critical. The enemy would be descending upon them with no mercy.

Bard bit back the shock his body took and passed a rifle to Tru. "It's loaded. I wouldn't wait to shoot. These guys live for killing."

The window beside Bard blew in to prove his point.

"Get down!" Tru yelled, and shot out over Bard's head. A quick glance showed a man flying backward from Tru's bullet.

"Thanks," Bard said. "I'll get the next one."

"You know it, buddy." Tru's forgiveness meant the world to Bard, and if they died today, he would go content, knowing they fought together. "We're going to get her out."

Bard bit back the tears and nodded his agreement. "For Luci."

Both brothers responded simultaneously, "For Luci."

From there, the three men took up arms and a post, and gave every shooter that ran their way the taste of their own vileness. Bard kept Hero down on the floor and out of the continuous spray of bullets.

"God," Tru said, his voice coming through the microphone. "We ask You to reverse the direction of every bullet. Cover us with Your shield and send the enemy running away."

"Amen," Jett and Bard responded, taking two more shots.

Bard noticed there were only a few shooters left, but he also was out of bullets. "I'm empty," he announced.

Tru said, "Same. Now what?"

Jett peered out above the window. "They're retreating."

Bard lifted up a bit to see out, questioning the reason for their departure. "I guess your prayer worked."

Tru said, "Prayer always works, but still prepare for retaliation. Whoever's in charge isn't going to like losing this many men from their crew."

"Then it's time to go. The element of surprise is on

our side." With that, Bard slid open the door and whistled for Hero. His dog jumped out, rippling with excitement to do what he did best: catch some bad guys.

SEVENTEEN

The second the bullets began to fly, Luci could no longer pretend to be unconscious. Those were the men she loved out there. Her brothers, Bard and even Hero were fighting for their lives. They were fighting for hers. How could she remain still?

"She's awake," the man in the passenger seat jumped from the car and opened the back door. He reached his fat hands in to grab hold of her by the shoulders, dragging her out headfirst. He dropped her to the ground, knocking the wind from her lungs. Pain from her bound wrists caused her to cry out.

Luci rolled over as fast as she could, getting to her knees to crawl toward the ambush. With her hands behind her, she fell on her face. She knew getting near the helicopter was a risk to her life, but to lose any of her men wasn't an option. Her brothers were everything to her, and Bard…was more.

Oh, why didn't they stay away?

"Let me go!" she yelled as the man grabbed her by the back of her hair, yanking her head back to look up at him. She searched frantically for the other guy, but he was nowhere in sight.

"Not so fast. You have some things to pay for." The guy who had a hold of her wore a grotesque smile of blackened teeth as he stooped down and picked her up like a rag doll. He threw her over his shoulder, and all Luci could do was kick. He grabbed her legs and squeezed them together, hurting her further where her legs had been cut from the window. Once again, she wondered why Jett hadn't turned back. For twelve years, her family had left her behind. Why did they have to start now to change their ways?

Squirming in the man's arms did nothing. He carried her into some sort of barn. She struggled to lift her head to see her surroundings, and then suddenly, he threw her. Luci had only a second in the air to prepare for the impact of hitting the floor on her side. She landed on her arm with the bullet wound and screamed as every one of her extremities cried out in pain. She heard her air escape from her lungs on a rush and struggled to refill them.

Rolling over onto her stomach eased the pain from her arm and allowed some air to return to her lungs, but she still couldn't think clearly. She wondered if she hit her head and struggled to open her eyes.

"Why?" she said in a whisper. "What do you want with me? I'm a nobody."

"Oh, don't be so hard on yourself. Everybody's somebody to someone." It was a new, unknown voice, and she sensed the man coming close to her to stand over her.

Luci rolled her head back and forth on the wood floorboards. "I'm not. I barely have a family. I'm easily forgotten. If you think you'll get something for taking me, I'm afraid you'll be let down."

"There's only one thing I want, and you're the only one who can give it to me."

Luci realized this was the buyer of her paintings. She had hoped to use it as a bargaining tool with the driver. She wondered if there was still a way. She had a feeling this was the end of the road. Once she told this man where it was, he would have no reason to keep her alive.

Unless…she wondered if it was even possible. "I'm assuming you're Fred Miller."

"I've been known to go by that name, yes."

She tried to lift her head and look behind her. The strain was too much, and she dropped her forehead back down again. "You're the one who bought all my paintings. Why?"

"I like them," he said simply. She felt the man pull on her wrists. Hearing the click and feeling her arms go limp, she realized he unlocked the handcuffs. "There. That should feel better. So sorry about that. We had to make your arrest look believable. That federal investigator with you would have smelled a rat."

Luci frowned thinking about Bard. Was he still alive? If she wasn't so weak, she would run and…what? She was useless. Useless to save him or herself.

But that didn't mean she was dead yet. As long as she had breath in her, she could hope to be free. Plus, she wasn't buying what this buyer was selling. "You didn't like my paintings. You destroyed them. You knew they were worthless, and nobody would miss them."

She heard footsteps on the floor and the scraping of the chair sliding up to her right. Next, she heard the chair creaking as the man sat down. When she turned her head, all she could see were expensive, shiny shoes and perfectly pressed gray pants.

"Actually, only the first one was destroyed. You saw that one in the cabin. Such a shame. But I have all your others…intact. I'm only missing one. And it turns out, it's the one I need the most. But first, I have to know, why did you steal it back?"

There was no use pretending the *Lady in Red* didn't exist. But that didn't mean she had to give up the painting's location.

"I didn't paint her right because I didn't see her correctly. Every day I passed her by while she sat in the Plaza. I ignored her. I was no different than anyone else. At first, I believed what everyone said about her. That she was befuddled and senile. And then after you bought the painting, I went out to find her, but she was packing up to leave. I tried to talk to her, but she only looked at me strangely and walked away. It was in that moment that I knew I got her eyes wrong. There was nothing befuddled in them. I realized I didn't see her—not who she really is—and I knew how that felt. Not to be seen. To be invisible and misunderstood. I had to fix her. I couldn't let her painting go out into the world like that. I've never stolen anything in my life. But I had to do it. I planned to return it by morning."

Luci felt defeated. She was where she was at because she stole the painting.

"What did you do to her eyes?"

"I filled them with knowledge. I showed the wisdom she has, that everyone who passed her by missed out on. That I missed out on."

"Sadly, I missed it too," the man said quietly. "I never miss any details, but I missed this one. That is why it is critical that I get this painting. I need to rectify my mistake."

Luci couldn't follow the direction of his thoughts. "Why would having this painting fix you not seeing her?"

"Because she's a witness. I passed her by, just as everyone else, like you said. I never saw her face, but she saw mine."

Luci heard remorse in the man's voice. But what was he sorry about? Was he sorry that he ignored her? He'd said she was a witness. But a witness to what? Had the woman seen him smuggling drugs?

That had to be it.

The full weight of the realization of why he really wanted this painting hit her harder than the floor had. In an instant, Luci forced herself to roll onto her back and look at who she was speaking to.

"Who are you really?"

"Darral Lindsay."

"Lindsay?" This was Lindsay?

"Like I said, Fred Miller is one of my names I go by. Aliases come in handy. Sometimes it's better to be invisible. It allows me to remain anonymous."

Luci pushed up to sit. "Except she saw you. You knew she saw you and you've been looking for her since. That must make you nervous. She can ID you. And not just for drug smuggling. She saw who you really are. The lowest of the low."

In a split second, the man backhanded her so hard that she fell back to the floor with a thud. Luci let a moan as she tried to catch her breath.

"If you thought we were friends, you were mistaken, Miss Butler. In fact, I don't let even my friends speak to me like that. Now, I'll give you one more opportunity to tell me where this painting is. And I mean only one."

She knew if she told him where to find that painting, the real lady in red would be dead within hours. She also knew the lady, who no one gave a moment's notice to, would be the only one who could tell what happened to her. Luci wondered if the woman realized how important she was. She wished that she had another chance to tell her.

"Well? What will it be? Will you tell me now or will you die instead?"

Luci licked her lips and, with every bit of strength she had left in her, lifted her head and spit on his shiny shoes.

Darral Lindsay jumped to his feet and, in one move, lifted his foot above her head.

Bard didn't even have to tell Hero to attack, but when Darral Lindsay saw the dog coming at him, he lowered his foot from Luci and drew his weapon to shoot.

Bard yelled to his dog. "Halt!" They had just raced inside the barn to find the criminal about to stomp on Luci.

Hero came to an abrupt stop and circled back to his owner. As Bard put his hand on his dog's neck, he kept his eyes on the man. It took every ounce of strength in him not to run to Luci to make sure she was still alive. His chest heaved from the exertion of running to this barn from the helicopter. Being well-hidden, it took them longer to find it from where they went down.

Was he too late?

In the next second, Tru and Jett ran in behind him. They came to a quick stop, but then Tru raced around Bard, yelling, "Lindsay! It's me you want. Let my sister go!"

"Not a chance." The man took out a handkerchief from his suit coat and wiped at his shoe. "You're about to find out what real pain feels like." Lindsay jerked his head to his right, and in the next second, men with rifles stepped out of every shadow in the room.

Bard could see the ambush on the helicopter was just the first troop. This one that guarded the main cell of the operation was three times as large. Two men approached Tru and forced him in a chair. They took up their positions beside him with their guns pointed directly on him.

Tru had dared to take down one of Lindsay's operations, sending the man's loved ones to prison. Now Darral Lindsay would make him pay by taking away *Tru's* loved ones—and forcing him to watch.

Bard's gut twisted at the heinousness of this man and what he had in mind. Lindsay sought out Luci and chose Salazar Gallery for this very moment.

As two guards descended on Jett, and two more came Bard's way, he put his hands in the air. "Lindsay," he said calmly. "I'm a federal agent who can make everything go away for you. Free the Butler family and name your price. I'll see that it's done. Whatever you want."

Lindsay tilted his head as he looked to be considering the offer. He smirked. "As impressive as that is, I'm going to have to pass. I do have to commend you, though, for figuring out my plan. You knew I would go after the weakest link of the family."

Bard scoffed at his remark about Luci. The man had no idea what he was talking about.

Lindsay narrowed his eyes. "Is something funny, Agent Holland? You won't be laughing when I shoot your dog."

Bard sobered instantly.

"That's more like it. You should've stayed out of this, Agent Holland. Now you'll be part of their punishment." He nodded to the muscle beside Bard. "Muzzle the dog and seize the fed."

As the guards descended on him and Hero, Bard prayed silently. *Lord, I could use some of that divine unexpected reversal that Tru asked for, because these are way too many bad guys for me to take down this time.*

Bard watched the men put a zip tie around Hero's snout, and his dog began to jump to fight back.

"Sit," Bard commanded for the dog's own good. Thankfully, he listened. Bard needed to form a plan, and he would need Hero to carry it out. Two men led Hero to the other end of the barn, toward a room at the back. As Bard watched to see where they were taking him, a car door slammed outside.

"It's about time you got here," Lindsay said to someone behind Bard. "Did you find it?"

"Sure did." Sal's voice pulled Bard from his dog. He spun around to the little man again. "But I don't know why you want it. It's horrible." Sal held up the painting of Luci's *Lady in Red*.

Bard lunged for the man before his guards could stop him. "How could you, you traitor?"

At the same time, Luci pushed herself up and ran at Sal. "Noooooo!" She was so quick that Lindsay's fingers missed their grasp when he reached for her. And when the first gunshot went off, it missed her and took out one of Tru's guards.

"Kill her!" Lindsay ordered.

With the other men distracted by the one guard down Luci ran for the painting in Sal's hands. She was out the door with it before anyone could take aim.

"After her!" Lindsay shouted in near hysterics. "I want that painting. Now!"

Bard looked at his dog getting put into the room. Time was critical, but Bard was certain that God had intervened. "Hero, guard Luci," he commanded. With that, the dog broke free from the men's grasps and ran at full force out the door. His long, lean body practically flew through the air in the long strides he made in his run.

As the men with guns burst from the barn after Luci and Hero, the race was on to catch the thief again. This time, as Bard and Luci's brothers fought off their guards, Bard yelled from the top of his lungs, "Run, Luci!"

EIGHTEEN

Luci knew she had only a few seconds before the men either caught her or shot her. As she raced out of the barn, she took a sharp right and made it around the barn before anyone exited behind her. From there, she headed into the trees for cover.

She could hear shouts and orders being given behind her, but she dared not look back. Every footfall echoed in her head, and her lungs burned with the exertion of pushing her pained body past its limits. In her left hand, she clutched the canvas in a death grip. She knew she would have to destroy it herself. There was no way she could lead Darral Lindsay to the real lady in red. Luci knew she didn't have much time to do away with the painting. At any second, she expected a bullet in her back. But with no direction through the wilderness, she didn't know where she could dispose of it. It wasn't enough to toss it into the river, either. It needed to be shredded and beyond repair, so the lady's face would never be recognizable. Luci made the decision that if she had to die today, she would make sure this woman was protected.

As she ran, the sound of panting came up behind her.

She knew before she saw Hero that he was now beside her. A quick glance to her right and she saw his snout bound by a zip tie. He had to be struggling to keep up such a fast pace with his jaw forced closed. She wanted to stop and rip it off him, but there was no time. She was grateful to have him beside her, regardless.

Luci ran on, ignoring the pain in her side that threatened to double her over. At times she led Hero, and other times, she knew he was guiding her.

When she saw the cave, a bit of hope surfaced. It was marked off as closed and hikers were prohibited from entering, but she ignored the signs and sought refuge inside, tripping over her feet in her last steps.

It was long and narrow in the beginning but opened up about twenty feet inside. A few rocks were scattered in places on the ground, but it was mostly flat and open. Once behind the shadows, she collapsed in sheer exhaustion, dropping the painting beside her. It would have to wait until she regained some energy.

Hero circled her before landing above her head and placing his snout on her arm that lay limp on the cave floor. He snuffled, and when she squinted through the slits of her eyes, she found him watching her intently with his dark eyes. It was like he was asking her to help him.

Luci tried to reach for the zip tie that bound him, but she had no energy. Her arm fell back down, useless. She heard whining, and realized it wasn't the dog but her. After a few deep breaths, she tried again. This time, she managed to get her fingers under the plastic and shimmy it down off his snout until finally he was free.

She opened her eyes fully in the dim light and saw

she must've cut him because the hair at his nose was red. "I'm so sorry," she said.

Hero leaned over and licked her face, bringing a small smile on her own. Just a few days ago, she was afraid of this dog, just as she had been his owner. But twice now, Hero had come to comfort her and showed her she had nothing to be afraid of. In fact, she could call him a friend. First in the makeshift shelter Bard had made her, Hero had let her use him as a pillow, and now in this cave where she would surely die, he let her know she wasn't alone. The shelter may give her a reprieve for a little while, but she knew the men would eventually find her and kill her. She couldn't let them hurt him too.

With the last of her energy and her good arm, she pushed the dog away. "Go," she commanded in the strongest voice she could muster. "I don't want you here."

It was a lie, but it had to be said. She had already caused so much death when she stole this painting. She couldn't cause any more.

But Hero only stuck out his long tongue and panted as if he thought this was a game.

"Go! Now!" She left no room for doubt that she was serious.

Hero jumped to his feet and ran around in a circle. She reached for the only thing around her and threw it toward him.

The painting just missed his hind legs, and the dog raced out of the cave.

Luci dropped her head back onto her arm, telling herself it had to be done. But that didn't make it feel any better.

I have to keep going.

Luci pushed up onto her elbows and then her knees. With her hands right in front of her face, she could see the discoloration of something on her fingers.

Blood. And a lot of it.

She didn't think she had cut Hero's nose that much. But if it wasn't his blood, then it had to be hers. She wondered if she had been shot, and in her high adrenaline didn't realize it. It would explain her weakened state. But upon inspecting herself, she only found the one gunshot wound in her right arm that she already had and the cuts on her legs. She knew her face was bruised from hitting the floor when Lindsay had struck her, but she didn't feel any blood.

So where did this blood come from?

She couldn't worry about it right now. She needed to destroy this painting, first and foremost. After all she did to hide it, she couldn't believe that it was Sal that brought it back. But then, why would she expect anything less from the man now? He had already proved to be a traitor. He used her for his own gain. And now he proved that he was no better than these criminals.

Tears threatened to spill, but Luci bit them back. She would not spill one tear for this man. She told herself that he didn't deserve it, but it still hurt. As she lay on this cave floor, and after all the death and violence she had witnessed, she wished she'd never met Salazar Ramon. She wished she never walked into his gallery last summer to see if he would carry her pieces. Little had she known that she had walked right into the lion's den.

A deep, throaty growl from somewhere deep in the cave lifted her face to the darkness. She apparently had walked into someone else's den as well. But would this predator be as vicious Sal?

As Luci crept backward toward the exit, she grabbed the painting and stood up. She turned around to run, but didn't make it two steps before she ran right into a man with a gun.

"Give me the painting, and I'll let you live."

It was the driver of the car, but instead of her making a deal with him, he was calling the shots.

Bard punched another assailant, ripped the gun from his hands and then used the butt of it to knock him out. He fell to the ground like the last three. Jett and Tru continued to fight their attackers, and Darral Lindsay was now in a fast retreat.

The man ran toward that door where the gunman had been bringing Hero. Whatever that door led to was a way out.

"I have to go help Luci," Bard said to her brothers.

"Go! We got this!" Tru yelled as he took a punch in the gut.

Bard thought about rushing in and helping them, but Jett whipped around and knocked out the man on his brother.

The two brothers could help each other.

Bard raced for the door but had no idea which direction Luci had gone. As much as he hated doing it, he whistled and then waited. He had wanted his dog to guard her, but right now, his dog was the only way to find her. He knew taking one step could send him into an ambush with the men spread out in the woods. He could only pray that his dog would make it back unscathed.

And that Hero wouldn't leave her unprotected.

A few gunshots rang out somewhere in the forest, and Bard's stomach clenched at the sound. He was tempted to go in the direction of the blasts. But suddenly, Hero jumped out from behind the barn in the other direction. He ran so fast that he passed by Bard and had to circle back before he could slow down.

Bard bent down and patted his dog. "Good boy," he praised him. He gave the dog a moment to catch his breath. Hero panted with exertion, but before Bard could tell him to take him back to Luci, Hero took off running again, back in the direction he had come.

Bard set out, doing his best to keep up with his dog. A few times all he could see was a flash of his tail as he turned a corner or ran around a tree, but he pushed himself because he knew time was critical. Luci was quick on her feet, but not fast enough to escape a bullet. And she wasn't strong enough to fight these men if they got their hands on her.

Please, God, I pray that that hasn't happened yet. I pray that You will get me there in time before they hurt her…before they kill her.

She had what they wanted, and once they had it in their hands, there would be no reason to keep her alive.

Bard's breath caught and his heart ached with more guilt than he had when he arrived in Santa Fe. Every choice he had made up to this point had come from that guilt. The fact that she was in more danger now than she had been when he arrived, he could tell that working from his guilt wasn't working. But he also couldn't expect God to step in and reverse what these men were doing when guilt was still what drove him.

And yet it felt different. It didn't feel like guilt that

kept his feet moving toward Luci. Letting Tru down may have set him in motion toward her in the beginning, but it wasn't what kept him going now.

So then what was it?

Before he could figure that out, a loud shout to his right cut into his thoughts, and just as he turned his head to see a man running at him, the butt of a rifle came down.

Bard fell to the ground in a skidding slump, gripping his head from the impact. Instant nausea overcame him, and his ears rang with a high-pitched noise. He grabbed hold of both sides of his head as the man kicked him in his side. His eyes flashed with a blinding light, and he couldn't see where his assailant was. All he could do was feel him attack from all sides.

Bard crouched into a ball, knowing if he couldn't see, he was done. And that meant Luci was as well.

Off in the distance, he thought he heard Hero barking ferociously. Then the kicking stopped but only to be followed by a gunshot.

"No!" Bard forced himself to stand, nearly falling over multiple times. With the blinding light, he had no idea which direction to move in.

Then he heard his dog attack and the man screaming, "Get him off me!"

Bard breathed a sigh of relief that his dog hadn't been shot. He dropped to his knees, feeling on the forest floor for the gun. When his hands hit the barrel of the rifle, he pulled it close and felt his way to ready it to shoot.

Slowly, the blinding light dimmed, and he could make out the blurry image of his dog holding the henchman down. He dragged himself over to stand above the man, and as Hero held him down, Bard searched him and removed a knife and a pistol.

"Thank you for these." To his dog, he gave the command, "Hero, release."

As soon as Hero jumped off, the man pushed back, turned and raced away, a blur. Bard figured he would be back, but not for a little while.

Hero raced around him, obviously still excited and wanting to go find Luci. Bard reached down to his collar and held on.

"I'll need to go a little slower," he said. He still couldn't see. The whole forest blurred in front of him, but at least he wasn't in complete darkness or blinding light anymore. The searing pain in his head hadn't subsided completely, but enough for him to think clearly.

Bard kept the automatic rifle in front of him with one hand and his other hand on Hero's collar. His dog kept pace with him and used his body to guide Bard's thigh in the direction he should go. They walked for what seemed like a mile. Luci had come farther than he had thought. He shouldn't have been surprised; he smiled, thinking of her spryness. Even wounded, she was quick.

And then he heard her.

He stopped for a moment and turned an ear to the sound of her voice. She was talking to someone. The tone of her voice seemed casual as though she was speaking to a friend.

It made no sense, as her brothers were back in the barn, and he had Hero with him.

So who was she talking to? Or more importantly, what was she saying?

"I know what it feels like to want to be important," she said, her voice trailing to his ears. "I know when

recognition is what we chase, we risk aligning our-
selves with the wrong people. I'm guilty of it as well.
You don't have to do this. You don't have to work for
people like Lindsay anymore. I know you think if you
give this painting to him, that he'll let you go, but you're
lying to yourself. That man doesn't care about anyone
but himself. Sure, he might give you a bonus, but you'll
still be just a number to him."

"I could do a lot with that bonus." A man's voice fil-
tered to Bard's ears. One of Lindsay's lackeys.

But he hadn't killed her.

Whatever Luci was saying to him, had him holding
back his trigger finger.

Bard crept closer to the mouth of a cave and stood
off to the side. He instructed Hero to sit quietly and to
wait for his command.

"I need that bonus," the man continued.

"Yes, I heard you mention you wanted to buy a
house," Luci said. "For you and… Rita?"

"I thought you were unconscious." A threatening
tone in his voice had Bard nearly running in.

"I was in and out," she said on a rush. "I heard a few
things only. But I heard that, and I also heard your part-
ner threaten to kill you and Rita."

"That's why I have to kill you. It's you or me, and it
ain't gonna be me."

"It doesn't have to be either of us. I trusted the wrong
person too. A good friend tried to tell me that, but I
wouldn't listen to him. And now here I am, standing at
the end of your gun. If I could only go back and let him
help me, I would be safe. If I only let him do his job in
the first place, things would be different."

Bard frowned hearing the remorse in her voice. He

wanted to rush in there and tell her that at any moment he could have taken control of the situation and arrested Sal like he wanted to. This was not a weight for her to bear.

"How do you know he'll help me?"

"Because he's the most honorable man I've ever met. He's strong and capable, and I feel so protected when he's near."

I'm right here, Luci. I'm not far from you at all. I'm so proud of you right now.

Bard wanted to tell her out loud, but it wasn't safe. One wrong move, and that trigger would be pulled. Bard vowed, however, to make sure she knew she was an amazing woman who was just as strong and capable, if not more than him. Here she was helping a man who had her at gunpoint, and she remained calm and collected.

"But that doesn't mean he'll help me," the gunman said. "He's a fed. He'll arrest me instantly, and I know I'll be killed in prison."

"Bard is only interested in getting the mastermind. That's not you. He wants Lindsay and Sal. They're the ones running the show. Do you know why they want this painting?"

"No, and I don't care. All I know is that painting is my ticket out of here."

"You're wrong. This painting is of a woman who can identify Lindsay. They will kill her by nightfall if they get their hands on this."

Bard felt his mouth drop open. It all made sense now. They needed this painting to tie up loose ends. Lindsay had all of Luci's paintings except this one, and it was the most important because he stood to be identified as the criminal he is.

"She's guilty of nothing but seeing the man walk into

a gallery," Luci said. "If they will kill her for something as simple as that, they're not letting you go anywhere."

Bard heard silence follow, and he wondered if Luci was getting to the man. The whole situation could turn on a dime, and Bard knew he couldn't wait much longer.

She said, "It's okay to admit that you aligned yourself with the wrong person. I didn't want to do it either, but now that I have, I'm able to make this right. You can too. Bard is a good man. You can trust him."

"You're sure about that?" The guy was wavering.

"I know it deep down in my heart. His size may make him look lethal, but he doesn't use his strength to intimidate. He uses it to protect people from those who want to harm them."

"And you're sure he'll help me?"

It's time, Bard thought. He stepped inside, gun pointed and saying, "She's sure. And I will. Just put the gun down and step away from Luci."

The man swung around, and Bard waited for him to pull the trigger, but instead, he did as Bard asked and dropped the gun. He put his hands up.

"They're going to kill me."

"I'll do my best to make sure that doesn't happen." Bard made the promise and hoped he could keep it. At the moment, he couldn't even see in front of himself. He kept that secret quiet. If the man thought he had been compromised, this could go south real fast. He was grateful that the sun behind him put him into a shadow, so his face couldn't be seen. He wasn't even sure if he was pointing in the right direction. "I'm sorry I have to do this. Hero, hold."

In the next second, his dog raced past him and pounced

on the man, knocking him to the ground and holding him there.

Bard stepped up with careful movements, feeling his way. When he reached the man, he kicked the gun away. Then he felt around to search him for any other weapons.

"I have the zip tie that had been on Hero's nose. Can you use that to tie his hands?" Luci held out something to him. Not wanting to let the man know about his sudden blindness, Bard felt for what was in her hand.

"It's perfect." He slipped the man's hands in and pulled it tighter, securing him. He stepped back and reached for Luci. His first attempt met nothing but air. Then he felt her reach for him, and he pulled her close. He dropped his cheek to the top of her head, breathing her sweetness in and telling himself that she was safe in his arms.

But for how long?

He felt her hand on his cheek, and she forced him to look at her. She was nothing but a blur, and yet she was the most beautiful woman he'd ever seen. It killed him to know he could not protect her outside this cave. If he stayed with her, he would put her at more risk. He would be a weight around her and hold her back.

"I want you to take Hero with you," he whispered.

"I'm not going anywhere without you." She reached behind his head and pulled him down to her face. He could now make out her eyes so close to his.

"Luci, I can't see," he whispered and dropped his forehead to hers. "It's not safe for you to be with me now. Everything is blurry and dark. All I can make out are shadows."

He could hear her short, sharp breaths as she processed this information. "Oh, Bard. How?"

"Hit in the head hard a little while ago and it was one time too many, I guess."

He felt her touch his scalp gently. He reached for her hand and brought it to his lips. It felt sticky and instant concern flooded him. He wanted to search her, but he couldn't see enough to know if she was injured.

She must've sensed his panic, because she said, "I'm okay. I don't know where the blood is from, but it's not me."

"Thank God. I need to get you out of here and back to your brothers. They'll be able to help you. Staying in here is too dangerous. These guys will find you, and you'll be cornered."

"There's an animal of some sort back there too."

"Then definitely, I want you to take Hero and make your way back to the barn."

"No," she cut him off. "I'm not going anywhere without you. I already said that, and I meant it. I just spent the last half of the year following a man who led me into this mess. You're the only one I will follow now, blind or not."

"I know a way back to the barn that will come in the back side," the man on the ground said. "I can lead you there."

Bard didn't see any other way, literally. "I'm emptying your gun."

"Fine. But you'll have to protect me."

"I'll tell them you were taking us back." It was the most logical explanation, and Bard found the man's gun and emptied the cartridge. "Hero will be watching your every move. Just in case you decide to change your mind."

"I'm destroying the painting," Luci said. "I need to find something to tear it to shreds. Right now."

"Are you sure?" Bard asked. It had to kill her to do such a thing.

"I can't risk anyone getting their hands on this painting and finding this woman. I won't allow it."

Bard reached into one of his pants pockets and removed the knife from the man who had hit him over the head with the rifle. He passed it over to her, feeling her hand to make sure she had it.

"When you're ready. And after, keep the knife on you."

Luci turned away with the painting and the knife. He didn't want to rush her, but when no sound came to alert him to her cutting into it, he said, "They'll be here soon, Luci."

"The painting is wet," she said in a confused voice. "I need a little more light." She moved past him to the mouth of the cave before he could stop her.

"Don't go too far. You'll be an easy target for a shot."

Her footsteps told him she kept moving forward until she gasped. "I don't believe it."

Bard walked slowly toward her, retracing the steps he took in. "What is it?"

"This isn't my painting. This isn't the *Lady in Red*. I mean, it's a lady and she's dressed in red, but it's not *my* lady. I don't know who this is. And the red paint on the edging is wet. As if it was painted…today." Lucy's hand reached out and grabbed his forearm. He knew now the stickiness was paint and not blood. "Sal didn't bring my painting. He created a fake and brought it. What does this mean?"

Bard huffed at the brilliance of this man. "It means

he played Darral Lindsay. And it means he's trying to protect you." Bard knew Sal was bad, but that didn't mean he was all bad. "It means you saw the good in him. But Luci…" Bard paused to think things through. Something didn't add up.

"What is it? Tell me the truth. I trust you to know what's best."

He smiled down at her. "You honor me."

"Because I love you," she said matter-of-factly. So matter-of-factly that he wondered if he heard her words correctly. Had he misunderstood?

But then, this was Luci, and nothing ever held her back from doing or saying what she wanted. It was part of her strength and character. But love? She *loved* him? Bard didn't think he'd ever had anyone love him. Sure, he had plenty of dates and short relationships, but no woman had ever told him that she loved him. He never let it get that far. Love didn't happen for people like him. Law enforcement was his life. His dog was his companion. He moved around following wherever the bad guys went. One case to the next.

"Now you really honor me," he said. "But don't let yourself love me, Luci. You deserve a family where you will never feel invisible. I can't promise you that kind of life."

"I didn't ask you to promise me anything. But I also don't hide my feelings. And I can't change them, and I won't even try." With that, she took the knife and sliced into the painting. She dragged it across horizontally and then vertically. Slice after slice ripped into the canvas until it was nothing but shreds. "I figured out your concern about Sal's move," she said. "Once Darral had the painting, he would kill me. Sal either didn't realize that, or he wanted him to."

"What do *you* think?"

"It doesn't matter what I think. I've been wrong this whole time."

"Or I have," Bard said. "Part of me wants to give Sal the benefit of the doubt and say he didn't realize they would kill you once the painting was found and turned in."

"Why are you changing your mind about him?"

"Because you see people. You know what it feels like not to be seen, and you make sure you don't do that to others. You say you trust me, but I also trust you."

"I didn't see the lady in red."

"But you *did*. Enough to paint her. And then enough to go back and fix her where you got her wrong. Luci, trust your instincts. They haven't steered you wrong. What's the bigger picture?"

"He killed his wife," she reasoned.

"Did he?"

She hesitated. "Well, not directly, but by being involved in this operation. You said he killed Cody Jemez, and when you accused him, he didn't deny it."

"Think bigger. Go outside the picture if you have to."

"What are you getting at?" She put her hand on his chest and leaned in so he could see her better.

"Who shot Natalie the first time?" Bard began to put the pieces together himself. "And why? What if they came to kill her because she could—"

Luci inhaled sharply. "She could identify Darral Lindsay! She told us that! She even said she would help me by testifying. She knew who the buyer was. She said she was in the gallery the night he came in to get one of my paintings."

Bard nodded. "And then what happened after she told you this?"

Luci gripped tighter to his shirt, making a fist. "The shooting spree."

"Which left her…"

Luci whispered, "Dead." She fell into him as if all the energy in her body went out. He wrapped his arm around her and pulled her close. "Sal was protecting her because he knew they were coming for her. He knew that because they already tried to through Jemez. Sal must've stepped in and shot him and then brought his body back to his apartment before coming to the cabin to hide with Natalie." Luci lifted her face to him. "Did we lead them right to her?"

Bard shook his head. "Don't go there. They would've found her eventually. You can't blame yourself."

"How can I not? You saw Sal's face when he realized everything was happening because I took the painting off the wall. He knew I put this whole thing in motion."

Bard cupped her face and lifted it to him. "The only thing he knew was that his crime had caught up to him. It was payday, and you just happened to get caught up into it. I didn't see anger on his face. I saw remorse. He never wanted to hurt you."

After a few quiet moments, she said, "You think I can trust him then?

"I think you can trust yourself to know that answer."

Luci nodded her head against his chest and, after a deep breath, straightened away from him and said, "We have to go back to the barn and get him. We can't leave him with that despicable man."

"I don't want you going anywhere near that barn."

"You don't have a say. You need my eyes."

"I can't argue with that."

"Bard, you tell me you trust me. Now prove it."

"It's not you I don't trust. It's them."

She lifted the shredded canvas pieces. "I'm the only one who knows who this woman is. Without the painting, they're going to need me alive still."

NINETEEN

The walk back to the barn, by way of an alternate route, was slow and quiet. Her driver-kidnapper, who Luci now knew was named Ruben, led the way with an unloaded gun in his hands and the zip tie still in place. She was surprised that they met no one on the way. She wondered if her brothers had anything to do with that.

"We're here," she said to Bard beside her. She walked with her hand looped through his arm. "How's your vision?"

"As the sun goes down, it's a little less painful to keep my eyes open."

"Meaning, you still can't see," she whispered.

Hero walked along Bard on his other side, guiding him with his body. His ears perked straight up, and he sniffed the air.

In the next second, her two brothers stepped out of the woods with guns pointed on Ruben.

Jett said, "Get on the ground."

Ruben complied, dropping his weapon and showing his tied hands. "They said they would help me"

Tru responded, "Is that right? Luci, care to explain?"

Bard cut in, "I'm willing to make a deal with him.

He got us back here safe and sound. What happened after we left?"

Tru stepped up in front of Bard and stared into his face. "Is everything all right, buddy?"

"I took a hit to the head with the butt of a rifle. It's probably just some swelling. I'll be fine."

Tru huffed. "I'll believe that when the doctor says it." Tru looked to her. "Stay by his side."

"Always," she responded and made both her brothers look at her with a question in their eyes. She wasn't about to tell them she loved Bard. But it felt good to have their attention for a change. Typically, she had to beg for it. Still, it was none of their business. "Just tell me where Lindsay is."

"He's inside with Sal," Tru answered. "Once we disposed of our guards, we were able to get out. We had radioed for help in the helicopter, but this is such a remote area, it could be days before help finds us. I think we take our chances and start walking out."

"Not without Sal," she said.

Tru looked at Bard who only nodded. "Are you sure about that? He's the one that got you into this."

"I know, but I also know it wasn't on purpose, and he tried to protect me as best he could. I have to go in and help him. They killed his wife. I'm sure he'll be next."

Tru looked at Jett, and at both their nods, she knew her brothers would be beside her. "Count us in," he said.

Jett said, "There's no way we're letting our little sister have all the fun. I'm trusting you remember those fighting skills we taught you? Things could get ugly in there."

Luci fought back a wave of tears. It was the first time Jett had referenced their childhood. She knew his amnesia had been healed and his memories returned, but he hadn't talked with her about anything he remembered from before the accident.

"I didn't know you remembered me. I mean, I knew your memories came back and you knew who I was, but I didn't realize you remembered such small details about me."

Jett stepped up to her and wrapped his arms around her. "Little sister, I remember everything, but I especially remember you were the glue that kept our family together. I remember the day you were born and how our whole family adored you. The day you came home and Mom put you into my arms was one of the happiest days of my life."

Luci let go of Bard's arm and wrapped both of hers around her oldest brother for the first real hug in twelve years. She closed her eyes and let this moment strengthen her for what was to come. She wasn't invisible, and she had a place amongst her siblings.

"I'm really the glue that keeps us together?"

Jett laughed and looked over at Tru. "When Tru called me and told me you were in trouble, I said, 'Without Luci, our family is done for.' You're not just the glue. You're our hope."

She sniffed. "Does this mean you'll come to my picnic?"

She felt his chest rumble against her. "Gatherings are still hard for me, but yes, Nikki and I will be there. My wife has been begging to reconnect with you. She always cared about you and never minded you tagging along."

Luci realized that perhaps Jett's avoidance of her gatherings had nothing to do with her and everything with him still trying to find his way after not knowing who he was for ten years. "Is that why you had a private ceremony last year? You struggled with gatherings?"

"Yeah, just us on top of our mountain. I'm sorry. It was all I could handle when my memories started coming back, and we didn't want to wait any longer. Ten years apart was enough." Jett smiled sheepishly. "Forgive me?"

"Absolutely. I'm so glad you found your way back to Nikki. I didn't realize how hard gatherings were for you. I'm sorry for that."

"They're exhausting. Every person I meet, I have to process memories and refile them again. But it's something I have to get over. I promise to do better."

"Me too, Squirt," Tru said. "But if we're going to go in there and get Sal out, we need to do this now while the troops are still in the woods looking for you."

Luci reached a hand for each of her brothers. "Having you both come to my rescue has been the greatest gift you could have given me. Thank you." She squeezed their hands, and before she realized what they were doing, they leaned down and kissed her on each cheek.

Jett pulled back and smiled. "I remember doing that too. Now let's go get your friend."

As her brothers walked ahead with Ruben to learn the layout inside, Luci put her hand back through Bard's arm. He leaned down and kissed her on her forehead. She remembered the last time he had tried to do that.

"Bard, I have a confession to make," she said.

"Now?"

"Better late than never." She started walking and leading him toward the barn. Knowing that once they entered anything could happen.

"Okay, spill. Confess away."

"When we were at your apartment, and you leaned down to kiss my forehead." She paused.

"What about it?"

"Without thinking I lifted my face to kiss you on the lips. I'm sorry."

They walked on for a few moments in silence. When she looked his way, she found him pressing his lips and fighting a smile.

"What's so funny? I'm trying to be honest here."

"I know you are. And I knew you kissed me."

She tilted her head his way. "You did??"

"Yes, Luci. I knew. It was the moment that I realized how brave you were, and I hoped you would never change that about yourself." His smile fell from his face. "Even if right now, I'm wishing you weren't so brave. Are you sure you want to go back in there? No one will fault you if you don't. I, for one, would rather you didn't."

"I know I'll be okay because I have my gentle giant beside me."

He looked down at his dog. "Do you mean Hero? You can count on him."

"I was talking about his owner, but I know the two of you come as a package. I'd say I'm getting a deal. Two gentle giants for the price of one." She led Bard along to wait for their orders from her brothers.

The sound of a gunshot had them all ducking. Then Luci realized it had come from inside the barn.

"Sal!" she said, running in blindly.

"Luci! No!" Bard reached for her but was too late. He took off in a run, but the lack of vision slowed his steps. Jett, Tru and Ruben went ahead of him, but Ruben paused outside the door.

"I can't go in there," he said to Bard. "I'm a dead man."

"Did you see her even hesitate?" Bard demanded from the weak man, showing him what selflessness looked like.

"No, but…"

"Are you afraid? You chose this business. You have no right to be afraid now. You knew what you were getting into. And now that woman is paying for it. She didn't ask for it like you. Go ahead. Run. But if you want my help with law enforcement, you'll stand and fight with us." Bard led Hero inside, leaving Ruben to make a choice. The man had to know he wouldn't get far if he ran, but that would be up to him to make another choice.

As soon as Bard stepped inside the barn, he could hear Luci crying. The sound twisted his stomach into knots. Heart-wrenching wails echoed to the rafters. It broke his heart to hear the pain coming out of her. And it could have only meant one thing.

Sal Ramon had been on the receiving end of that gunshot.

The light was dim inside the barn, making it harder for Bard to see even more. He squinted to make out figures of Luci's brothers standing over her.

Tru approached him, whispering, "We're too late."

"Sal?" Bard asked.

"One shot to the head. He's dead."

The fact that they were out in the open told Bard that the shooter was either gone or dead as well. With the rest of the crew still out looking in the woods, Bard figured the shooter had to have been Lindsay.

"Where is he?" he asked Tru. It was critical that the man was found, or his friend would never have peace. Darral Lindsay would forever be coming after him to make him pay for putting away his family.

Bard wanted the man for personal reasons, namely the pain he had caused the woman he…*loved*? That was not a subject he was ready to dissect. Did he even know what the word meant? Luci seemed to know, but the idea seemed more like a fairy tale, and he didn't believe in fairy tales. Fairy tales meant suspending reality, and he didn't do that. He dealt in facts; things he could see.

He couldn't see love.

And yet, as he heard her weep, he saw everything plain as day with his heart. He saw how he wanted to spend the rest of his days comforting her and supporting her, even if it meant he had to chase her down as she went after her dreams.

And if he had anything to say about it, she would succeed in being a sought-after painter, known for her talent.

"He was gone by the time we got in here," Tru responded. "The place is empty."

"The tunnel," Ruben said. The man had decided to come in after all. "He comes and goes through the tunnel. I don't know where all the passageways lead to."

Bard thought of the short leg through the tunnel that he and Luci walked through. He knew two stops on the path. Who knew how many there were? Lindsay would have an advantage.

But Bard had Hero.

"I need something of his," he said to Ruben. "Did he leave anything behind?"

"I don't think so. I don't see anything." Ruben searched the area. He reached down and picked something white up. "It's a bloody handkerchief. But I don't know who it belongs to."

Luci came near. As she closed in on him, he could hear her sniff back tears, but when she spoke, all he heard was anger. "That's his. I spit on his shoe after he smacked me. It's my blood, but it's his cloth. He took it from his fancy suit coat and wiped off his shoe with it. Bard?" Her voice cracked. "You have to find him. You have to make him pay. For killing Sal and Natalie and for hurting you. But how can you find him if you can't see?"

"I don't need to see. Where I'm going, it's dark." He took the handkerchief and bent down to Hero. Putting the cloth under his dog's nose, he said, "Hero, seek."

As he held on to his dog's collar, Hero put his nose to the floor and started sniffing rapidly. As soon as he caught the scent, he picked up his pace, pulling Bard into a half run toward the door to a room off to the back. It was the door they were going to bring him into, and to who knows where they would have taken him. Bard supposed the drug operation could use a drug-sniffing dog to protect their assets.

"Wait!" Luci called from behind. "I'm coming with you."

Bard didn't bother telling her that that wasn't a good idea. He knew she would do it anyway.

"We're coming too," Tru said, stepping up on the other side of Bard with his brother. Ruben could be heard racing to catch up. The man wasn't about to be left behind.

"It's a narrow tunnel. The dog goes first," Bard said.

Tru checked his gun. "I swiped some ammo from a dead guy. I'll be covering you, Bard."

It felt good to have his friend back. "I appreciate it. I wouldn't want it to be anyone else."

Tru may be a ranger at Carlsbad Caverns National Park, but he knew how to handle a weapon. Being so close to the Mexican border, he had his own fair share of smugglers to apprehend. He also knew his way around dark caves, so this tunnel wouldn't faze him in the least.

"But who's covering Luci?" Bard said under his breath.

"Jett has our little sister covered. She's too important to lose. Without her, there's no hope for the Butler family."

"Stop talking about me like I'm not here," Luci said. "But thank you." She said the last part with an obvious smile that Bard could hear in her voice.

As Hero sniffed his way down the stairs to the tunnel, Bard realized they could all die if Lindsay started shooting. At the base of the stairs, there were three routes to take. Hero sniffed around until he made his decision.

Straight.

From that point on, no one said a word. They didn't want to alert Lindsay to their presence. The man might start shooting into the dark. Knowing that he could take them all out before they even got close to him had Bard second-guessing having Luci there. The idea of holding her lifeless body had him slowing down, tugging on Hero and holding him back.

She asked, "Is everything all right?"

He felt her hand on his back, and it made him catch his breath. "I don't want anything to happen to you. Luci, I want you to go on to become a famous painter. This dark world of crime could steal that from you faster than any painting being ripped off the wall. It's already stolen so much from you. All your hard work."

"They can steal my paintings from me, but they can't steal my passion to create more."

"But what if they steal you from me?" His fear slipped from his lips.

"Oh, Bard. That would be impossible. You're stuck with me. Just ask my brothers how annoying I could be, following them around wherever they went."

Jett laughed. "Luci, I don't think the man thinks of you like an annoying little sister. I don't think he thinks of you as a sister at all."

As they filed through the tunnel, two by two with Jett and Ruben at the rear, they pushed them closer to each other. Bard could feel Luci behind him. He reached his free hand back and found hers in the dark. He may not be able to see her love for him, but the way she entwined her fingers through his showed him what a life linked with her would be like.

"Jett's right," Bard said. "When I think of you, I don't think of you as a sister. And when we get out of here, I'm going to kiss you to prove it."

"Promise?"

Before he could answer, Hero started barking, which meant he'd found what he sought, or rather who. But in the next moment, multiple gunshots blasted through the tunnel. At least one of them took Bard down as he heard his dog attack.

Bard fought against true darkness as he felt his life seep from him.

TWENTY

When Bard went down, Luci went with him. She kept a hold of his hand as chaos ensued around them. She could hear Hero growling as he held Lindsay on the ground. She could hear the despicable criminal screaming in pain as her brothers fought and apprehended the man. And she could hear Ruben worrying that he'd lost the person who would get him his bargain. But none of those things were as loud as her own mind screaming about losing this man she loved.

Luci felt his torso for where the bullet went in. When she found nothing, she feared the bullet hit his head.

"Ruben, I need your help. We have to get him out of here. I can't lift him."

The man lifted Bard under his arms while Luci held his legs. They made their way back toward the barn and finally made it up the stairs. As Ruben exited the door with his back facing out, Luci noticed the place swarming with FBI agents. The real ones.

"Help him!" she yelled. "Please, someone. He's been shot."

Now with some light, Luci could see the side of Bard's head bleeding. But before she could assess the wound, men in FBI coats surrounded him. More went down the stairs and met her brothers and Lindsay.

Luci collapsed onto the floor, but first Bard was whisked away. Soon, an irate Darral Lindsay was taken away into custody. Then someone stood over her, asking her questions, but Luci couldn't process anything the man said.

She tilted her head and tried to focus on his words coming out of his mouth. It took him three tries before she understood that he was asking her if she was Lucille Butler.

"Y-yes, I a-am." Luci realized she was trembling with shock setting in.

"You'll have to come with me for questioning." He offered her an arm to help her stand. It was a nice gesture, but she didn't think he was just being kind.

"What do you want?" she asked bluntly as he led her from the barn with his hand on her elbow.

"We have some paintings that belong to you," he finally said as he put her into a car. All around, she saw agents leading men out of the woods in handcuffs. It was over.

So then why was she being taken away too?

"I didn't do anything wrong. I had no idea Sal was using my paintings to smuggle drugs."

"Do you have anyone to corroborate that statement?" He stood outside her door.

"No…" She looked back at the barn and saw her brothers running out to her. "They're all dead. Sal's dead. Jemez is dead. Natalie…anyone who could tell the truth is gone. But I'm telling you the truth. I knew nothing about it."

"Get her out of that car right now!" A loud voice bellowed their way, causing the agent to turn around.

Luci thought it had been one of her brothers, but she couldn't see behind the tall agent until two hands gripped his arms and moved him out of the way.

Then Bard stood outside the door, reaching in for her, grappling until he found her hand.

"Bard!" She latched on to him, having to touch him to be sure what she was seeing was real. "How?"

He had blood streaming down the side of his head and pooling in his neck, but he was alive.

Barely.

Luci felt him tilt into her, and she knew she couldn't hold him up if he went down.

He didn't answer, but rather squinted in the direction of the agent. "She is innocent in all of this, and she will not be going anywhere with you or anyone else."

"Sir, I'm sure you understand that I must investigate her involvement with this operation. I would not be doing my job—"

"Your job is to arrest the bad guy, and you got him. Thanks to her."

"Her name is on those paintings." The agent grew louder. "From where I stand, it looks suspicious."

Bard stepped closer to the man, moving Luci behind him. "Let me give you a short lesson, from one agent to another. Things are not always as they appear. Learn this now before you hurt innocent people."

The man looked ready to explode. His face turned a bright red, and anger morphed on his face at Bard. "You can't stop me from doing my job."

"On my jurisdiction, I can, and I will. This is BLM land."

The agent looked around Bard and locked a warning glare on her. "Don't take any vacations for a while." With that, he turned and shut the back door, walking away.

Bard said to his retreating back, "And we're going to need those paintings back. In perfect condition."

The man scoffed and shook his head. "They're evidence. I can't promise you—"

"But you'll do your best," Bard finished for him with a daring tone. "Also, Ruben deserves leniency. He helped us take Lindsay down."

The agent huffed and left them, and Bard's legs buckled instantly. He had held out just in time. Luci wrapped her arms around his waist, trying to hold him up, but it was a lost cause.

Suddenly, her brothers were there, taking over. "Let's go, buddy. Back in the ambulance," Tru said, holding him from one side with Jett on the other.

"Luci!" Bard called.

She ran around the front of them and moved as close to him as possible so he could see her. "I'm right here. I'm not leaving you. Ever." And she meant it.

They reached the ambulance, and the paramedics waited with the stretcher that Bard had been on before. Blood covered it but he lay back on it with the help of Jett and Tru. Immediately, he reached out his hand, and she took it.

"I'm going in the ambulance with him," she said but stepped back for the paramedics to lift him inside.

As she waited to climb up, Luci felt her brothers' hands on her shoulders. She quickly turned around and wrapped her arms around them both. "Thank you for coming to my aid. You have no idea how much this means to me." Tears threatened to spill as her throat thickened.

"You never have to ask, Luce," Jett said. "We're family."

"That means even more." She looked up into Jett's cut up face. He took a lot of hits today and could have died fighting for her. "And I'm so sorry about your helicopter."

He smiled and winced. "Yeah, that one hurts. But it was worth it. *You* are worth it, little sister." Jett leaned down and kissed her forehead.

"Sure are, Squirt," Tru said, pulling her in for a tight embrace. "I promise to never ignore your calls again. If I didn't learn anything from all this, I definitely learned that. And now, because of you, our family is safe from the Lindsay family, once and for all. Danika is safe, and I will be forever grateful to you and Bard for that."

Luci smiled. "I look forward to meeting her." Luci pulled back to see his face. "You're bringing her to the picnic, right?"

"Yes, but I'm also bringing Mom and Dad." He raised his eyebrows in warning.

She sighed. "Of course. I suppose it's time."

Jett nodded to the ambulance. "It's time to go."

"Wait!" Bard yelled, trying to sit up.

A paramedic pushed him back. "Sir, the bullet may have only grazed you, but you have a severe concussion. And you've lost your eyesight."

"My dog. I need my dog." He attempted to whistle, but nothing but air came out in his weakened state.

Luci turned toward the barn and gave the whistle call she had heard Bard use with Hero.

Somewhere inside, the dog barked ferociously. Shouts could be heard to stop him, and then suddenly, Hero burst out the door in a leaping run toward them. He ran three circles around Luci before she pointed for him to jump inside the ambulance.

The paramedic jerked back in obvious fright at this large dog coming his way.

Luci let her brothers help her up. "Don't worry. There's nothing to be afraid of. He's a sweetheart." Luci smiled down at Bard. "And he's my hero."

Bard laughed and reached for Luci's hand to pull her close. He kissed her gently, saying, "And you're mine."

Suddenly, a cold nose pushed in between them as Hero rested his head beside Bard's and snuffled.

"You better get used to it, boy," Bard said, looking at Luci. "Because I love her, and she's not going anywhere." With that, he closed his eyes with the most peaceful expression she'd ever seen on him.

"Sleep, my love." She brushed his cheek. The man hadn't stopped protecting her since the moment he saw her steal her painting. When any other cop would have handcuffed her and arrested her on the spot, he protected her instead. "You deserve it more than anyone else. And I love you too."

TWENTY-ONE

Rain poured down at Luci's new apartment complex, effectively ruining her picnic. She had wanted everything to go so smoothly, but with the rain, her family would need to be inside the small space. The problem was she didn't have a chair or table or anything for them to sit on. She had nothing but her box of memories that Bard had helped her salvage at her studio.

Bard.

Just thinking about him calmed her nerves. He promised to be here, though she hadn't seen him since he was discharged from the hospital three days ago. Since then, Luci had said goodbye to Cody's mom who moved back to her childhood town. Mrs. Jemez was so distraught over her son's crimes. She really never knew he was involved in such behavior. Luci was also glad to see Ruben was being given a deal for testifying against all the remaining criminals in Lindsay's ring. But nothing made her happier than when she went by the gallery and saw the lady in red had moved on to another street. She was also wearing blue instead. Luci felt sure that the woman would be safe now. As far as where Luci would live, she rented an apartment in the same complex as Bard.

If he ever came home, he would see it.

She found his absence odd. He still couldn't see, and she wondered if he would let that come between them. The doctors said his brain was so swollen, it could be a few months before the pressure was relieved enough for clear vision. There was a possibility that his eyesight would never return, but she would worry about that another day. And she would not let him push her away because of it.

Not today when any minute her brothers, their significant others and her parents would be arriving. It would be the first time she would be with them all together since her brother's memories returned. Her stomach did a little flip at the thought. It was her own fault, she reasoned. Somewhere along the way, she had become a bit of a recluse, telling herself she was getting lost in her art. Perhaps she was just as guilty of avoidance as her parents.

Luci checked the time on her phone. They were all late. Paranoia whispered that no one would come, even while the rain was most likely the reason for their tardiness.

She walked to the counter and opened the box of her childhood memories—the only belongings to her name. She flipped the cover of the small photo album to a family picture on the ski mountain in Taos. None of them had any idea they would split apart and go their own ways soon after this shot was taken.

For years, Luci looked at this picture and prayed for her family back. Was she about to see that prayer answered?

The doorbell rang, and she left the album on the

counter to answer the door. Tru and a tall, athletic woman with long brown hair stood on the doorstep. She leaned into Tru, and Luci saw how the two of them were perfect for each other.

"Danika?" Luci said, reaching for the strong, beautiful woman who had given her brother a reason to live again. "Thank you," Luci whispered as she hugged the woman, even if Danika had to bend down to receive it.

"I'm so glad to finally meet you," Danika said. "Tru has told me everything about you. I feel like we're already sisters." The woman's eyes shined bright. "He said you were cute for a little sister, but you are stunningly adorable."

"What do brothers know?" Luci rolled her eyes at Tru, who planted a quick kiss on her forehead. Then he said, "Nice place you got here. Spacious." He looked around at the empty room. "Where's Bard?"

Luci shrugged. "He's not here yet. I'm not even sure he's even coming, actually."

"What?"

"He said he had some things to take care of after he left the hospital. His sight hasn't returned, and I'm worried he might be experiencing some depressive episodes. I want to help but he hasn't been at his apartment." She nodded across the parking lot. "Not that I've been watching."

"Sure you haven't."

Luci saw her parents coming up the walkway, dodging the rain. "You didn't tell me they were here already."

"We drove over together. They were parking the car. We're staying with them while we're in town. They're nervous. Go easy, okay?"

Luci had already made up her mind how she would

treat her parents when they arrived. Twelve years was too long to hold on to anger. They were in pain, and they acted out of that pain. Out of everything Sal taught her, that was his biggest lesson to her. People make poor choices in their pain.

As soon as her mom stepped foot into the foyer, Luci launched herself at the woman, wrapping her arms around her. Her mom inhaled at the shock but quickly let out a heart-wrenching cry. Minutes went by as mother and daughter made up for the lost years.

When Luci pulled back, she saw her father's face streamed with tears. "Do I get one too?"

Her dad was much taller than her mom, but Luci wrapped her arms around his waist and pressed her cheek to his chest. She closed her eyes to the rhythm of his heartbeat and let it lull her into contentment.

"You couldn't wait for us?" Jett's voice bellowed as he and his wife, Nic, ran up the walk, getting drenched in the rain. Nic's two red braids swung out as she and Jett rushed up the steps, hand in hand.

"You've already made amends with them. It's my turn," Luci said, letting them inside.

He leaned down and kissed her forehead. "Fair enough, Luce. You remember Nikki?" He beamed bright at his wife with such adoration.

When they were younger, Jett had called the pretty-but-tough redhead *Nikki*, and it was so good to hear him call her by that name again. It really meant he was back…after so much loss. Back then, he and Nic had no idea the accident would split them apart and send her away to find her own place as an FBI agent. But now, here they were, together again, forever, and ever.

Luci's heart expanded for this woman who had been

such a huge part of her brother's life before the car crash, but an even bigger part now as his wife. The pain Nic had experienced must have been unbearable when the man she loved didn't remember her. As she took Luci into her arms for a strong embrace, Luci realized she wasn't the only one forgotten. That everyone in this room knew the feeling of being invisible. Perhaps everyone in the world at some point in their lives knew the feeling.

As Luci closed the door, she took one more long look in the direction of Bard's place.

He wasn't coming.

Whatever he had to do didn't include her. Even though he had said he loved her, he also warned her before that not to love him. Was this why? Did he know he wouldn't stick around?

When Luci joined her family in the kitchen, they were gathered around the photo album on the counter, flipping through the pages.

"I can't believe you have this!" Tru exclaimed. "This is great stuff. Look at us! I remember this day. We hiked Wheeler Mountain, and I broke my arm trying to scale a cliff."

"Glad to see your rock-climbing skills improved. Sort of." Danika sent a joking smirk his way.

"But you still love me," he replied, leaning in to kiss her quick.

As they found joy in the memories of past years, Luci took in the family before her. The rain streaming down the windows didn't seem to bother any of them as they went through her pictures. It seemed exactly what everyone needed today.

She took out her phone from her pocket and snapped

a few shots, wanting to remember the first day she got her family back. They may all look different and were living out their own lives that God had planned for them, but Luci never had to think she was inconsequential to any of them ever again.

Still, she knew this picture wasn't right.

Two things were missing.

But this time, Luci had to accept the fact that she couldn't fix it.

Just then, a hard bang on the door echoed through her empty apartment, followed by a bark.

"I knew he'd show up eventually," Tru said, winking at her. "Aren't you going to answer the door? He sounds impatient."

Her family waited with expectant gazes. Their wide eyes of excitement made her cheeks flush. She waved them off and went back to the door, barely breathing the whole way. Forcing air into her lungs, she drew deep and let it out slowly as she reached for the doorknob.

Swinging the door wide, all she saw was a gigantic brown box in the air.

Glancing around it, she spotted Hero sitting beside two legs in tactical pants. "Bard? Is that you?"

"I come bearing gifts. Guide me in, and I'll show you. Hurry the box is getting wet, and I don't want them to be ruined."

Luci stepped back, not sure how to help him with such a cumbersome load. But he moved past her and put the box down in the middle of the empty living room. Her family had now congregated in the doorway to see what Bard had brought.

"Hello, everyone," he said to the crowd. "Gather

around. Hero, sit," he ordered when his dog started sniffing the strangers.

But all Luci noticed was Bard had *seen* Hero do that. Or maybe he heard his dog sniffing. That had to be it.

Bard opened the box at the top and reached in with two hands. In the next second, he lifted a canvas and looked at it. "This one's nice." He scanned the room and brought it to lean against the wall by the front window.

Luci knew her mouth was hanging wide open as he returned to the box for two small paintings. He placed them on the empty fireplace mantle.

"Bard? I don't believe it." She heard tears in her voice.

"Yes, sweetheart, they're all here. I got them all back." He took out two more and leaned them against the wall behind him. Moving faster now, he removed the eight remaining in the box, holding the last one close. Slowly, he turned it and showed her the *Lady in Red*. "I even went back for her. I figured we could have a bonfire tonight and burn it. Don't want her to ever be at risk again."

"But Bard...you can *see*?" It was all Luci could focus on. She moved toward him, studying his gaze as she closed in. He didn't drift his gaze once but rather kept it locked on her.

"I can see better than I ever have before," he said slowly. "I see the beauty of your heart. I see the creativity of your mind. I see the talent of your hands. Darral Lindsay didn't destroy these paintings because he knew he was looking at true art. Luci, you are amazing." He looked around the room at her works displayed, but she put her hand on his cheek and drew him back to her.

"Look at me," she said. "Can you see me?"

He smiled and put the painting back in the box. She

expected him to reach for her, but instead, he bent low and got on one knee. He was so tall that they were almost at eye level.

"What are you doing?" she asked, unsure of the sudden turn of events.

He opened the palm of his hand to reveal a diamond ring. Picking it up with his other hand, he held it out to her. "Yes, I see you, and I love you. You have honored me so much already, but if you would give me the greatest honor of becoming my wife, I promise to see you for the rest of my life. I promise to see your dreams, and I promise to see all that you are that makes you uniquely you. You will never be invisible to me. Will you marry me, Luci, and give me the honor of loving you for the rest of my life?"

Luci heard a few gasps behind her but could only focus on her gentle giant in front of her. She nodded over and over again, letting him put the ring on her trembling finger. He stood abruptly, scooping her up in his arms and lifting her off the floor in one swoop. His lips found hers quickly for a kiss that literally swept her off her feet.

Cheers and claps and Hero's barking filled the echoing space as Bard twirled her around, laughing through his joyful kiss. When he brought her back to earth and lowered her to the floor, Luci cupped his face and stared into his intense gaze, feeling his love pour into her.

"Just so you know, I would have still said yes if you were blind," she said.

He kissed her gently on a sigh. "I know you would have, and that makes me love you more. But even if I was to lose my sight again, you would never be invisible to me. Because you have taught me to put my focus on the unseen and not just what my eyes can see. You have opened my eyes to the bigger picture. For that, I will always be grateful."

"No, that was God. I know because He did the same thing for me." Luci looked to her family. "The truth is I haven't wanted to see the bigger picture and that everyone had their reasons and pain to deal with. I hid behind my canvases." She looked around the room at her work. "But thank you for bringing them back to me."

"They would have been locked away forever and that would have been a tragedy. The world needs to see them. And they will see you too, Luci. I just know it in my heart."

"And when they do, they will see my gentle giant by my side."

Bard whistled, saying, "You heard her, boy. She wants you right beside her."

Hero came bounding over, circling them both before plopping down at their feet.

"Always and forever," she said, lifting up on her tiptoes to capture Bard's lips as he had captured her heart.

* * * * *

If you enjoyed this story, look for these other books by Katy Lee:

Holiday Suspect Pursuit
Cavern Cover-Up

Dear Reader,

Thank you for following the Butler siblings' journey to love and the lives God had planned for them. Trusting God with our futures can seem scary, but to know Him is to know He has great plans for His children.

Luci captured my heart with her spunkiness and her creativity. Her love of painting was inspiring to dive into. And Bard Holland deserved his redemption from letting his friend down in the previous Butler story. The two may not look equally matched, but in spirit, they were perfect for each other. She had just as much grit in her little body as he had in his towering one.

And let's not forget about Hero, the smart Belgian Malinois who was *my* hero! Between you and me, I think he might have stolen the show.

Thank you again for reading *Santa Fe Setup*. Be sure to follow me on Facebook or Instagram, and you can always contact me on my website: KatyLeeBooks.com.

Happy reading!
Katy Lee

COMING NEXT MONTH FROM
Love Inspired Suspense

ALASKAN MOUNTAIN SEARCH
K-9 Search and Rescue • by Sarah Varland

To rescue her niece, the next possible victim of a rogue killer, police officer Bre Dayton turns to the man who broke her heart. But teaming up with search and rescue worker Griffin Knight and his K-9 puts them all in the line of fire.

HER SECRET AMISH PAST
Amish Country Justice • by Dana R. Lynn

When a run-in with gunmen lands Joss Graham's mother in the hospital, Joss is sure that the danger may be connected to a cryptic note they received about a secret from the past. Can Sergeant Steve Beck keep Joss safe long enough to unravel the mystery of her true identity?

FORCED TO HIDE
by Terri Reed

Texas judge Adele Weston's courtroom explodes, and she barely manages to escape along with her staff. Deputy US marshal Brian Forrester must whisk the judge to a safe location in the Texas Hill Country without falling victim to the killers that are after her.

KIDNAPPED IN TEXAS
Cowboy Protectors • by Virginia Vaughan

When FBI agent Luke Harmon learns he has a teenage daughter, he'll do whatever it takes to rescue her from a human trafficking ring, even work with her mother, Abby Mitchell, the woman who hid her existence from him for fourteen years.

MISTAKEN TWIN TARGET
Range River Bounty Hunters • by Jenna Night

Taken by men targeting her identical twin sister, Charlotte Halstead escapes with the help of bounty hunter Wade Fast Horse. But when her sister goes missing the next morning, Charlotte convinces Wade to help her find her twin...even as they come under attack.

RANCH UNDER FIRE
by Tina Wheeler

Fleeing after witnessing a shooting in her office, Bailey Scott must rely on cowboy Jackson Walker for protection. But with a powerful killer on their trail, safeguarding Bailey may be harder than he anticipated.

LISCNM1222

HARLEQUIN
PLUS

Announcing a **BRAND-NEW**
multimedia subscription service
for romance fans like you!

Read, Watch and Play.

Experience the easiest way to get
the romance content you crave.

Start your **FREE 7 DAY TRIAL** at
<u>www.harlequinplus.com/freetrial</u>.

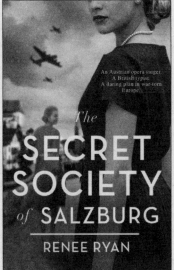